INSIDE AFFAIR

PRIME TIME SERIES #1

ELLA FRANK

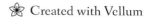

ALSO BY ELLA FRANK

The Exquisite Series

Exquisite

Entice

Edible

The Temptation Series

Try

Take

Trust

Tease

Tate

True

Confessions Series

Confessions: Robbie

Confessions: Julien

Confessions: Priest

Confessions: The Princess, The Prick & The Priest

Confessions: Henri

Confessions: Bailey

Elite Series

Co-Authored with Brooke Blaine

Danger Zone

Need For Speed

Co-Authored with Brooke Blaine

Sex Addict

Shiver

Wrapped Up in You

All I Want for Christmas...Is My Sister's Boyfriend

DEDICATION

*Sometimes the most interesting people are
right in front of you.
It just takes something monumental to make you see.*

~ Xander

1

XANDER

"THAT'S ALL FROM us here at Global News on this Thursday evening. I'm Alexander Thorne, thank you for watching and good night."

Aiming my familiar smile toward camera one, I watched the final words on the teleprompter disappear and then heard in my ear, "Aaaand we're out. You're all clear."

I nodded toward the cameramen, indicating we were good to go, then shut my laptop as the door to the studio was pulled open and Jim Berkel—my executive producer—walked inside.

With his headpiece still in place but the microphone now shut off, he crossed the floor with a tight expression on his exhausted face and tried for a smile, which he failed at miserably.

"Good show tonight. Nice work. Especially the A and C blocks. They were very smooth."

I gathered up the papers in front of me and eyed my EP

closely. Jim and I had worked together for nearly six years now, him in my ear feeding me the most important facts and information about some of the biggest news events the country had ever seen. But in all the time that I'd known him, I couldn't once remember him kissing my ass quite so spectacularly after a run-of-the-mill broadcast.

Over the last twenty-four hours, nothing catastrophic had happened, meaning the stories we'd run with tonight hadn't been last minute and the material had been well prepared. So the grim line to his mouth and stress lurking in his weary eyes could only mean one thing—something was up in house. Something I wasn't going to like.

"I agree, it was a good night. And as much as I appreciate your post-show wrap-up and review, why don't you stop buttering me up and tell me the real reason you're in here?"

"That is the real reason."

"Somehow, I sincerely doubt that." I pushed back from my desk, got to my feet, and pulled the earpiece from my ear. "You only ever rush in here after a show if I mess up or if Marcus is on the warpath—"

"Marcus wants to speak to you in his office."

Damn it. I hated being right. But if Marcus St. James, the president of the news division, wanted to speak to you privately, it was never about anything good. "Why?"

"Don't know."

"Do you really not know? Or know and just don't want to tell me?"

"Does it matter?"

Not really. If Marcus called, you answered—that was just the way it went, even if your name was number one in the news world. "Tell him I'll be up once I change."

"He said now."

Okay, then. I knew better than anyone else that if Marcus said jump, your only response better be: how high.

I unclipped my mic and earpiece and handed it to Jim as we exited the studio. Now that the night was winding down —well, our portion of it—the newsroom was a muted version of itself. Heads were bent over keyboards and eyes were glued to computer screens as everyone wrapped up their work for the evening, preparing to leave in the next hour or so. But as I passed by my assistant's desk, Ryan looked up and pointed his pen in my direction.

"Marcus—"

"Wants to see me, I know."

Ryan glanced at Jim, who was trailing my every step, and then added, "Yes, but he said alone."

Fantastic. That didn't bode well at all. This seemingly straightforward night was getting more cryptic and annoying as it went along. There were only two reasons a person was ever called into Marcus St. James's office, and one usually ended with the person never setting foot in the building again.

But I hadn't done anything wrong, not that I could recall, so what the Almighty upstairs wanted with me was anyone's guess.

"Right. Tell him I'm on my way up, then, would you?"

As I walked off toward the double doors of the news-

room, I heard Ryan call out, "Sure thing, boss." I pushed
through them and made a beeline for the elevators.

Marcus's office was two floors up, and as I got in and
punched his number, I glanced at my watch. It was just
going on six fifteen, and it was coming up on the end of my
workday.

When the doors slid open and I stepped out into the
hall, a wall-sized poster of my face with *Global News with
Alexander Thorne* splashed across the image greeted me. It
was the new promo that the station was rolling out for the
summer, and as I stood there sizing myself up, I decided
they hadn't done a bad job.

With my new studio set of the world highlighted in blue
and white lights behind me, it brought out my eyes and the
silver highlights of my dark hair. All in all, it looked classy,
sophisticated, worldly. In other words, exactly what the
network had been going for.

I headed down the hall to Marcus's office, passing by the
desk where Carmen, his assistant, usually sat. It seemed
she'd been dismissed for the evening, judging by the empty
seat and otherwise sparse floor, and as I reached his office
door, all I could think was *lucky Carmen*.

I took a second to brace myself, and then I knocked.

"It's open."

I pushed open the door and stepped inside the one place
in the building I actively tried to avoid, and when my eyes
landed on the man seated behind the ostentatious desk, I
waited for Marcus to look up and acknowledge me. He
didn't.

"You're late. The broadcast finished fifteen minutes ago."

My spine stiffened at the accusatory tone. His voice was that of a school principal addressing a petulant child, as opposed to the network and country's number one news anchorman.

When I didn't immediately reply, Marcus finally looked up from whatever it was he'd been reading and pinned me with an expectant look. But I'd be damned if I apologized.

"It took me a couple of minutes to un-mic and get up here."

"I see." Marcus pushed back from the desk and got to his feet, and at six foot and a whole lot of extra inches, he was an imposing figure to say the least. Add in his autocratic demeanor, cunning eyes, and golden head of hair, and he reminded me of a lion sizing up his next meal.

At forty-two, Marcus was considered young in the world of broadcasting. But that hadn't stopped him from earning a reputation for being cutthroat and tenacious when it came to his job. He had a stare that could cut glass and a disposition that left you ice cold, and in all the time that I had known him, I couldn't once remember seeing him smile.

"You had a good show tonight." The statement was more factual than complimentary, as he walked around his desk.

"I did." I left it at that, because really, I didn't owe him anything else. I'd been working at ENN for years now—nearly ten—and I knew my worth, just as Marcus did. So if he had an issue, or something on his mind, then he could damn well say it.

Marcus clasped his hands behind his back as he stopped in front of me. "There's no easy way to say this—"

"Then how about you just say it?" My frosty tone had Marcus narrowing his eyes, but after being summoned up here like a level-one intern, my patience was growing thin.

"Very well. A threat was made against you this morning on the station's website."

Okay. That wasn't what I'd been expecting. A thorough dress-down over something I did maybe, but... "A threat?"

"Yes."

Well, he definitely had my attention now. It wasn't like I hadn't had threats made against me in the past. I was an out gay news anchor, so it kind of came with the territory, whether it be about the stories I reported or my personal life. But what was different this time was that Marcus had called me into his office. He'd never done that before.

"That's nothing new," I pointed out.

"No, it's not. But the nature of this threat is, and this is the third one you've received in a matter of days. From the same person."

Hang on a minute. "There's been more than one? How did I not know about this if it's been going on for days?"

"There's been three, and the first one came in on Monday."

"Why wasn't I told then?"

"Because I wasn't convinced it was serious then."

"And you are now?"

"I am." Marcus turned to his desk and grabbed up the papers he'd been looking at. "Take a look for yourself."

I took the papers from him, zeroing in on the three messages that had been lifted from the ENN Twitter feed and emailed to Marcus.

MEANT2BMINE: *@AlexanderThorne. I saw you on last night's broadcast. You looking at me, telling me to have a good night, and I knew it was time to finally introduce myself. Time to come out from the shadows and say hello. So, hello, Alexander. I'll be seeing you soon.*

Message two.

MEANT2BMINE: *@AlexanderThorne. A venti redeye every morning before work. So that's how you make it through the long hours. I always wondered, you know. But that barista, Kyle? He's a little too friendly, imo. You might want to tell him that you're taken. Tell him that you're mine.*

I swallowed around the lump that had suddenly formed in the back of my throat and tried to squash down the rising bile. This guy was delusional. But even more alarming, he knew what kind of coffee I drank and where I got it from. How could he know all of that? Unless he'd been...following me.

But it was the last message that really made the hair on the back of my neck rise.

MEANT2BMINE: *@AlexanderThorne. Why are you making me wait like this? Playing the fucking tease? This distance you're keeping between us is killing me when you know we should be together! I want to touch you, be with you, Alexander. You're meant2bmine, and soon you will be.*

"As you can see, the last message is what concerns us the most," Marcus said, cutting through the panic that was now threatening to overwhelm me. "Whoever this is, the threats are escalating. The tone is much angrier. They want contact, a one-on-one interaction, and they know your address."

"Right..." I said as I read my home address on the tweet directly under the last. I walked over to look out the window to the buildings across from Marcus's office, and for the first time wondered who was over there looking back at me.

MEANT2BMINE? No, that was just crazy thinking.

"Look," Marcus said when I remained silent. "It's probably just some overzealous fan. But we're going to need you to take on some security."

"Some security?"

"Yes. *Some* is the wrong word, though. More like twenty-four-hour security until we work out where these messages are coming from and have them stopped. Don't worry, you're insured. It's all part of your contract."

It is? This was the first time I'd heard about it. Then again, I'd never had such a personal threat aimed at me before. Still, the idea of some random stranger following me everywhere... "I don't know that twenty-four-hour security is necessary. You're talking a bodyguard? That makes me uncomfortable. Plus, my building is secure—"

"I don't care."

"You don't care?"

"No. You're worth far too much alive for me to care about your comfort level here, Alexander. You need security until this is taken care of, and I don't give a damn how you feel about that."

I could tell by the square set of his jaw that Marcus

wasn't about to budge, and if I really thought about it, he was right. This person knew where I lived. They knew where I worked. And the idea that they'd been watching my every move sent a shiver down my spine.

"Fine. I'll hire someone, okay?"

Marcus opened his mouth to no doubt tell me the company would take care of it, but I quickly cut him off.

"I'm the one who's going to be spending all my time with them, so I should get to pick who it is." I immediately thought about my best friend Bailey and his boyfriend Henri's new PI company. They might be a good option. But the idea of asking either of them to move in and protect me when they'd just recently moved in with one another somehow felt wrong.

I supposed I could ask Sean, Bailey's oldest brother and total pain in the ass, for some advice. He was a detective with the Chicago Police Department and would no doubt have a few connections with personal security firms. But I wasn't at all comfortable with going to Sean and asking for help.

Yes, we'd known each other nearly all our lives, but we'd never had an easy relationship, more a relationship due to circumstance. I was in his brother Bailey's life, therefore I was also in his. But what other option did I have?

"I know someone who should be able to get me in touch with the right people," I said.

"Should be able to? That's not good enough."

"*Will* be able to."

"You need to get on this tonight. I want a name by tomorrow."

"Tomorrow?"

"Yes, tomorrow. Or you'll get whoever I stick you with." Marcus pointed to the messages on the paper. "This person is not fucking around, and you'd be smart not to either."

I nodded, understanding the severity of the situation even though I didn't want to.

"Okay, leave it with me." I fished my cell phone out of my pocket to look for Sean's number. "I'll have a name for you by tomorrow."

"See that you do," Marcus said as I headed for his office door. "Oh, and Alexander?"

"Yes?"

"Be careful who you trust. People aren't always who they appear to be."

I frowned but nodded as I opened the door and headed out into the hall, where I hit Detective Sean Bailey's number and waited for him to answer.

2

SEAN

"YOU NEARLY DONE for the night, Sean?"

I glanced over the partition between our desks to see Mick Callahan switching off his desk lamp and getting to his feet. I leaned back in my chair and winced at the stiffness in my lower back. "Yeah, almost. I got a few more things to log in to evidence on the Willow case, but then I'll be out."

"You need any help?"

I arched an eyebrow as Callahan grabbed his jacket off the back of his chair and shrugged into it. "And if I said yes?"

"I'd tell you to go ask Davies. I got a hot date tonight, and I ain't breaking it for you."

"Like I'd want you to." I returned my attention to my computer. "But I gotta say, it felt really fucking good getting that asshole off the streets today. Even if I did have to spend one too many months working with the likes of you."

"Eh, you loved every minute of it." Callahan stopped

with one hand on the door. "But don't forget to go home tonight. If not for sleep, to get a change of clothes. Those jeans and that shirt are about to walk right out of here."

"Hey, I wore these so I'd fit in."

"Sure you did. You even smell like you fit in. Night, Sean."

"Fuck off, Callahan."

Callahan's chuckle was muffled as the door swung shut behind him, and as his words rattled around in my brain I took a quick whiff of myself and was relieved to discover that he was full of shit. My clothes might've looked a week old and well lived in, but there was no lingering odor to them. If I'd been out there any longer, that might've been a whole different story.

Tonight's arrest had brought an end to a three-month case I'd been working with the guns and gangs unit, hence my shadow, Callahan. They'd been tracking down an illegal gun dealer that had left a trail of dead bodies along the way.

It'd been a long, round-the-clock case that had left little time for anything other than work, and after I logged in a gold Rolex watch—the final piece of evidence—I shut the file and ran a hand through my too-long hair. I'd let it go over the last couple of weeks, and decided the first thing I would do tomorrow was get it cut.

Jesus, I was tired, my lack of sleep and, well, life finally catching up with me as I looked at the clock and saw I'd put in yet another eighteen-plus-hour day. *Shit.* I switched off my computer and shoved back from my desk, my bones protesting as I unfolded myself from the unstable seat I'd been perched on for the last couple of hours filling out paperwork.

I needed a vacation. It wasn't often I thought that—okay, I'd never actually thought that—but as I pushed my chair under the desk and grabbed my phone to see two missed calls from Bailey, one of my younger brothers, I knew it was time.

I couldn't remember when I'd last seen my family or been able to attend one of our Saturday night dinners. I'd been so busy on this case that it had consumed all my time. But as I headed out to the parking lot, I decided I'd done the right thing in asking for some leave.

Around six months ago I'd come precariously close to hitting rock bottom. But after a *come to Jesus* talk from Bailey, I'd decided that maybe the bottom of a bottle wasn't the answer to all my issues and decided to just bury them in work instead. Now it was time to unwind.

I pushed the button on my key fob to unlock the door to my black SUV, and as I climbed inside and started the engine, my phone began to ring. I looked down at the screen and frowned at the name, but as Xander's number continued to light up my phone, my brain went into automatic panic mode. There was only one reason Alexander Thorne called me, and it usually had to do with my brother and Xander's best friend—Bailey.

Shit, maybe something had happened to him. Like that time Bailey had been involved in a shooting on the job.

I hit accept, and it connected to my stereo system. "Xander? Is everything all right? Is Bailey?"

"Hello to you too, Sean. I'm doing fine, thanks for asking. How are you?"

I narrowed my eyes on my phone but said nothing in response. Xander sighed.

"Everything is fine. Bailey is fine. As far as I know."

"What do you mean as far as you know?"

"Well, I haven't seen him since Saturday, and that was six days ago, so—"

"Xander." I rubbed a hand over my face. "Is Bailey okay?"

"Yes. I assume so."

"Okay. Jesus." I looked at the time and noted it was about an hour or so after Xander's broadcast. "So what's with the call, then?"

Xander coughed. "I, um..."

I frowned as I waited for him to continue. It was unlike Xander to be at a loss for words, but then again, it was also completely unlike him to call me...at all.

"I was wondering if I could swing by your place tonight and pick your brain about something."

Nothing he could've said would've shocked me more. I'd known Xander nearly all of my life. He'd always been in it in some capacity. First, as the skinny little kid next door, then as Bailey's annoying best friend, and later his boyfriend.

As far as I knew, they were back to the whole best friend thing since Henri Boudreaux had come on the scene, which seemed a little complicated to me. But as far as I was concerned, Xander had always just been there. You know, like another...brother, I guess.

"Swing by? You've never swung by my place, Xander. Do you even know where I live?"

"I will when you tell me." Xander paused, and I could've sworn I heard him mutter something before he spoke up again. "Come on, Sean. I need some advice and I don't want to beat down Bailey and Henri's door at night—"

"Why not? Worried you'll interrupt something?"

"No, I just don't want to bother them with this when I can ask you. Stop being a shit and help me, would you?"

I couldn't exactly pinpoint why, but Xander's pissed-off tone had my weary brain re-engaging. "Yeah, okay. *Swing* on by. I'll be home in ten."

"Sean?"

"Yeah."

"I need your address."

Huh, how weird was that? In all the years I'd known Xander, he'd never known where I lived. Guess he wasn't that much like a brother after all. Not that it mattered. Whatever was bothering him had to be something pretty serious if he was willing to drive his million-dollar self out into my neck of the woods. "I'll text it to you now. See you soon."

3

XANDER

THERE WAS ONLY one reason I ventured outside of the city and into the burbs, and it usually had to do with one of the Bailey brothers. Granted, it wasn't usually *this* Bailey brother, but since the other one was all but engaged these days, I'd decided to hedge my bets.

As I turned on to Sean's street and pulled into the short drive behind his SUV, I couldn't help but wonder if I'd made the right decision tonight. I hadn't seen Sean in a while, which wasn't anything unusual when he got a case. But the last few times we had been in contact, things had been a little...tense.

Sean was an "all work, no play" guy. The Chicago Police Department was the only world he seemed to know. I understood that, the "work hard and never stop" mentality, and I respected it. I was much the same. I'd had to be to get where I was today.

The difference, however, was that I knew how to stop.

When the news was done for the night, and I stepped out of the ENN building, I made sure I had a life. Friends, lovers, a world that wasn't always so serious. A world that had some kind of lightness and levity to it. Otherwise I'd wind up a cynical, jaded pain in the ass—which, of course, led me right back to Sean.

Not the most affable guy around, Sean Bailey didn't make it easy for others to approach, and while that probably served him well in his line of work, when it came to interpersonal relationships, it made things...difficult.

Those messages Marcus had shown me tonight made braving Sean seem worth it, though. They'd left me more than a little rattled, to where I'd all but strangled my steering wheel on the way over here, while looking in my rearview mirror like some kind of fugitive. And if swallowing my pride and asking for help was what I needed to feel somewhat at ease in my own skin again, then I'd swallow that bitter pill and beg Sean for a name and number.

Letting out a sigh, I climbed out of my Maserati and closed the door behind me. I wasn't looking forward to this. I hated asking for help, almost as much as I hated the idea of some bodyguard monitoring my every move, but Marcus wanted a name by the morning, and I'd be damned if I didn't get him one.

I smoothed my hands over the lapels of my suit jacket as I walked up a cracked concrete path toward the home. As I approached, a sensor light switched on over a plain white door, and I noted the few scraggly hedges around the entrance that had seen better days. Then, just as I was about to knock, the door was pulled wide open.

"Well, what do we have here? The illustrious Alexander Thorne standing on my li'l ole doorstep. To what do I owe this pleasure?"

I glared at Sean, and in that moment wished I'd had that final growth spurt that pushed me past his six-three frame. But no, Bailey and I had topped out at an even six, leaving Sean to lord it over us for the rest of our lives.

With shoulders broad enough that they just about filled the doorframe and an attitude pricklier than a porcupine's, I supposed Sean's overall appearance and demeanor helped when it came to his chosen career path. However, to those of us who existed in a world where we had to converse with others, it was a rare day that Sean didn't open his mouth and somehow irritate the shit out of someone close by.

That someone right now just so happened to be me. "Are you done? Did you get it all out of your system?"

Sean rubbed his fingers over the dark scruff covering his chin and shrugged. "Maybe? Maybe not. Come on, Xander. You got to admit, it's not exactly an everyday occurrence for you to rock up at my place in the shadows of twilight. What'd you do, kill someone?"

"No. Jesus. Would you just get out of the way and let me inside?" I took a step forward and shoved him in the arm, and Sean finally stepped out of the way.

"Okay, relax." He chuckled. "No need to get all pissy about it."

But as I walked into a narrow hall and stopped to see

him still standing in the open doorway, there was no relaxing in sight.

Ever since I'd left the news station, I'd been trying to push aside the nerves that had been building in me. I'd *tried* not to think about who might be watching me, who might be following me. But as Sean stood there with the door wide for anyone to see, a wave of panic rushed in, and I, well...I lost my shit. "Can you hurry up and shut the fucking door?"

Sean's eyes widened, and with a sharp flick of his wrist, he slammed the door shut behind him.

"Lock it, too." Sean opened his mouth to speak, but I quickly cut him off, not in the mood for any of his smartass retorts. "Just do it, Sean."

I watched closely as Sean not only engaged the lock on the handle, but also the chain, then he turned back to me and crossed his arms. "Okay, it's locked. You wanna maybe tell me what's got your panties in such a bunch tonight?"

"I don't wear— Shit. I just..." I ran a hand through my hair. "I just need to talk to you, and I'd rather not do it with the door open for the world to hear, if that's okay with you." When Sean merely stood there, I looked over my shoulder and down the hall. "This the way to your living room?"

"I guess you could call it that," Sean said, as I headed off in that direction. "Not that I do that much living in it."

I came to a stop in the sparse space and scanned the bare walls, lone recliner, and mounted television on the far wall. "I can see why."

"Yeah? Well, not all of us can live in a fancy-ass skyscraper, you know."

I totally agreed, and didn't actually think Sean would know how to enjoy the finer aspects of luxury apartment living. But this? This place was just depressing.

"You ever heard of a photo or coat of paint?" I took another look around. "Something to add a little bit of character to the place?"

"My bad." Sean came around to stand in front of me. "And here I thought we could sit around and discuss what kind of color scheme would go best with my complexion. I thought you were here for help, not to offer up your expert design skills."

"Can't I do both?"

"No, you can't. I just got off a long-ass case, I'm tired, and *you* called *me*. So what's going on, Xander?"

He was right. I *was* the one who'd called, the one who was inconveniencing him, and here I was being a rude shit.

What can I say? Sean always brought out the best in me.

"I need your help."

"Yeah, I kind of gathered that—"

"*Sean*, can you just for one second in your life not talk? Please."

Sean shrugged and kept his mouth shut—shocker. I swear, the guy could talk under water with marbles in his mouth. Always had an answer for everything.

"I need your help," I said. "I have to get some...personal security."

When Sean stood there mute, I glared at him, and he pointed to his mouth. It was official. I was going to kill him.

"You can talk."

"Are you sure?"

I gnashed my teeth together, and Sean smirked.

"Just checking."

"More like agitating. So? Can you help me out or not?"

Sean's dark blue eyes wandered over me. "Personal security, huh? I mean, I know you think you're a big shot and everything in the news world, Xander. But I hardly think people are mobbing you when you walk down the street for an autograph."

"Not that kind of— God, you're annoying."

Turning away from him so I wouldn't resort to something as juvenile as punching him, I wandered over to the small hole in the wall that I supposed could constitute for a window, and found myself thinking about who was out there. *Who* might be looking in.

Shaking off those thoughts, I quickly got back on topic.

"My station wants me to hire a bodyguard. Trust me, if I didn't have to, I wouldn't. But since I don't have a choice, I want to choose, and I thought that you might be able to help point me in the right direction of a company I could—"

"Wait a minute. Hold up." I turned to see Sean walking around the recliner toward me. "Why do you need a bodyguard? Is someone threatening you?"

I thought about those final lines I'd read: *I want to touch you, be with you, Alexander. You're meant2bmine, and soon you will be.*

I slipped my hands into my pockets to keep them from shaking and tried my hardest not to appear unnerved. "It's nothing, really."

Sean took a step closer and scrutinized my expression, searching for the truth. And for the first time since I'd entered his home, there was no joke lingering in his eyes. Sean looked one hundred percent serious.

"That wasn't my question, Xander. Has someone been threatening you?"

4

SEAN

I WASN'T SURE why, but the idea that someone had been messing with Xander made me want to ram my fist through a wall. Sure, we'd had our ups and downs in the past, but that was to be expected between people who'd been in each other's lives for as long as we had been.

But the thought of someone making Xander feel unsafe? Making him feel as though he needed protection when he walked down the damn street? Well, that just made my blood fucking boil.

As I waited for a response, Xander cocked his head so he could look me in the eye. I could see the indecision there, that confidence I knew he prided himself with faltering as he struggled with his next move.

Truth or lie. Truth or lie. He nodded.

"Yes, okay? There have been three threats sent to the station."

"Directly against you?"

He swallowed but kept eye contact. "Directly against me."

Shit, this was not good. Whatever had been sent had spooked Xander, and considering how put together the guy usually was, that had my senses tingling.

I rubbed a hand over the back of my neck, trying to decide how best to play this. But one thing I knew for certain was that I needed more information. "Has this kind of thing happened before? I imagine you get crazies every now and then, annoyed at what you're reporting or how."

"Right, we do. I've even gotten hate mail due to my personal life and choices."

"Because you're gay?"

He rolled his eyes. "You don't miss much, do you, sparky?"

"I'm just making sure we're talking about the same thing here so there's no confusion."

"Then yes, let me be crystal clear. I've had some pretty horrible comments based on the whole gay anchor thing, but this is the first time one added my address at the bottom and said, *You're meant2bmine and soon you will be.*"

"Fucking hell. That's some serious shit."

Xander grimaced. "I know, that's why my boss is demanding a bodyguard by tomorrow morning."

"As he should. You don't know what this lunatic is capable of. Do they want to kidnap you? Scare you? Keep you for themselves? Do they believe if they can't have you then no one else should?"

"Gee, that's so comforting, Sean. Thanks."

He didn't sound comforted. But hey, I wasn't about to lie to him. "I'm just pointing out that your boss isn't wrong. You need a bodyguard."

"Which is exactly why I'm here. Do you know a reputable company? Maybe someone you've worked with?"

I knew plenty of people, but I wasn't about to source him out. "Me. I'll do it. I'll come on as your bodyguard."

Xander sputtered a little, or maybe he was just clearing his throat. "Are you kidding? No."

If the topic hadn't been quite so serious, I might've found his incredulity amusing. However, there was nothing remotely funny about what he was telling me. I'd known Alexander Thorne most of his life, and I'd never seen him so on edge. These threats had shaken his usually cool exterior, and right now he looked as though he were about to go off the deep end.

"Why not?"

"Because I don't actually *want* people to know I have a bodyguard. Yes, I want this asshole caught. But if he sees you trailing me in all black with a scowl on your face, he'll go into hiding and we'll never find him."

Hmm, he had a point. But so did I. I'd wanted some time off from the force but knew a standard vacation was not for me. So what better way to occupy my time than taking on this as a side job?

"Okay then, what are you thinking? No matter who you hire, they're going to trail you. That's how bodyguards work."

"I know that." Xander clenched his jaw, clearly pissed

off about the whole situation, and I couldn't blame him. I wouldn't want someone observing every move I made. But at the same time, I also enjoyed being alive. "What if they—"

"*I.*"

"You're not doing this, Sean."

"I am, but we can discuss that after. Keep going."

Xander glared at me so hard that I was surprised lasers didn't come out of his eyes and melt me to the ground. But too bad; I wasn't about to let my brother's best friend hire some schmuck off the street when I knew I could do a better job. Xander would just have to suck it up and deal with it.

"What about undercover?" he suggested. "What if they come on as my assistant?"

I didn't miss his insistence that whoever he was going to hire wouldn't be me. But we could duke that out later—for now, we needed to get the details ironed out, and one thing I knew for damn sure was that I was nobody's errand boy.

"How about no? I'm not going to be your whipping boy for the next however many weeks, sorry. Next idea."

"It's not going to *be* you. So I don't see the problem."

"It is going to be me. So...next idea."

Xander mumbled something I didn't quite catch, then went to step around me as though he were leaving.

I grabbed his arm. "Where are you going?"

"I'm leaving. What does it look like I'm doing?"

I tightened my fingers around the expensive material of his jacket and shook my head. "Uh-uh, are you crazy? I'm not about to let you walk out that door after what you just told me."

"And what do you plan to do? Handcuff me to a chair?"

"If I have to."

"I'd like to see you try."

If he kept up this attitude, he just might get his wish. As Xander tugged his arm free, we stood there in a stalemate, and I noticed the slight flush to his cheeks.

Xander was usually put together—always ready for the camera, Bailey would say. But as he stood there now, his looks very much matched his mood—frazzled.

His sea-green eyes were wary, darting around at every little sound my house made. His gunmetal-colored hair was sticking out at all angles from the fingers he'd run through it, and the tic in his jaw was increasing in speed the longer we stood there with our horns locked.

He was clearly agitated and trying not to let it show with this bullshit bravado act, but it was time to let him know he'd done the right thing in coming here.

"Look, I know you weren't expecting to hire me for this job, but I'm not about to let someone else take this on when I know full well that I would be better at it. I've had years of experience undercover, I would have the full support of the force behind me to look into backgrounds, locations, and anything that might arise—plus, I know you. Bailey would never forgive me if I sent you away and something happened to you."

Xander's eyes roved over my face—God only knew what he was looking for—but then he let out a breath and nodded. "Okay."

"Okay?"

"Yes, okay. You're right. I'd feel more comfortable having you around than some stranger, so why not. But I still don't want you to *look* like my bodyguard."

"Yeah? Well, I'm not gonna be your assistant." When Xander rolled his eyes I added, "Plus, how would you explain me driving you to and from work every day?"

"That's what you're going to do?"

"That is part of the job. A bodyguard is there to *guard* the body. I can't do that if I'm not with you. So I'll have to come and stay with you too."

"*What?*" Xander's eyes widened until they all but encompassed his face. "You've lost your mind."

"I need to be with you at all times outside of work, and it needs to be plausible. So if I'm not your assistant, I could be, I don't know, a relative visiting from out of town? That's not too far off."

When Xander screwed his nose up, I ran through several other scenarios in my head until I finally landed on one I knew would be perfect, but also the hardest to sell.

Oh well, it wasn't like he could want to kill me anymore than he already did. *Here goes nothing.*

"Or if you don't like that, I could always pretend to be your boyfriend."

5

XANDER

"MY BOYFRIEND? YOU?" I took a step back, and when my legs hit Sean's recliner and I fell down into it, I decided that seemed like the best place for me.

Tonight had taken one strange turn after another, and honestly, this was the strangest of all. There was no way what he was suggesting could work. No way Sean could actually pull it off—me either, for that matter.

Sean and I barely tolerated each other under the best of circumstances. The idea of pretending to be a couple was just...just... "That is the most absurd idea I've ever heard."

"Why?"

"Because it is. You can't pretend to be my boyfriend. For one, you're straight."

Sean eyed me as he shoved a hand into his jeans pocket. "That's why I'm going to *pretend*. It's a job, Xander. Nothing more, nothing less."

How in the world Sean was suddenly the clearheaded,

rational person in this discussion was beyond me. But while I sat there trying to wrap my head around what he'd just proposed, Sean was off and running with it.

"If you think about it, it actually makes the most sense. And it's not like we don't know each other."

Okay, forget that. He wasn't rational. He'd lost his damn mind. "Sean, I know you've done this whole undercover thing before, but this is different. I'm not sure you could pull this off. Hell, I'm not even sure I could."

Sean scoffed. "How hard could it be? I stick close to you, I open a few doors here and there—"

"You're going to have to do more than that to make people think we're dating." I rubbed my temple, where I could feel a headache forming. "They actually have to believe you are sleeping with a man. You understand that, right? That's what you're suggesting we pretend. That you like touching a man, kissing one." I glanced at the hand by his side and brushed my fingers over his. When Sean immediately pulled it away, I raised an eyebrow. "Yes, I can see you'll be *very* convincing."

A deep V formed between Sean's brows. "You caught me off guard, that's all. I didn't realize we were starting this instant."

"Bullshit." Getting to my feet, I shook my head. "This isn't going to work. A person can't change their behavior overnight, and you flinching every time I touch you is not going to convince anyone that you're sleeping with me."

"That's what I'm trying to convince them? I thought it was that we were dating."

"And you don't think we'd be having sex?"

Sean ran his eyes over me, and I couldn't quite tell what was going on behind that stare. He looked deep in thought, almost contemplative. Then he stepped in close to me and reached for my hand.

As the warmth of his touch penetrated my skin, he grazed his thumb over the back of my knuckles and something alarming happened—my pulse began to race.

"What are you doing?"

A smile that I'd never seen before slowly curved Sean's lips as he continued to massage the back of my hand. "What does it feel like I'm doing?"

It felt like he was touching me in a way he never had, which was disconcerting, to say the least. Not to mention that teasing smile. Where the hell had that come from?

Clearing my throat, I went to pull my hand away, but Sean tightened his grip.

"Okay, Sean. You can stop now."

"Stop what?"

"This." I tugged our hands up between us and looked at the way his large fingers enveloped mine. It was a sure hold, a firm one, and the most intimate contact I'd ever had with him. "You made your point. You can let go of my hand now."

"Why? Is it making you uncomfortable?"

"No. Of course not." Although it was, very much so.

"Good, because if we're going to pull this off, you're actually going to have to look like you enjoy touching me, kissing me. You know, a man?"

As Sean's smile turned smug, I relocated my brain and

shoved him in the arm, yanking my hand free. "Are you done?"

Sean laughed, and any odd reactions I'd been having a second ago were replaced with irritation.

"Yeah. Just proving a point. When I'm in character, I'm in character. I think I can pull off pretending to like you to save your life."

"How reassuring."

"All I'm saying is, it's hardly a stretch. We're already friends, so it's not like we aren't used to being around each other. I'm sure we can put on a good show."

I'm glad he was so sure, because I still wasn't convinced. This was *Sean*, Bailey's annoying older brother. How in the hell did he expect me to stop thinking of him like that?

"I don't know, Sean..."

"Do you trust me?"

"What do you mean?"

"Do you trust me to look after you? Do you trust me with your life? Because that's the main question here."

As I stared into his earnest eyes, I knew this was one area in which I had no doubts. I did trust Sean. He was one of the most dedicated detectives in the CPD. He was ruthless, brash, and rougher than sandpaper around the edges. But I knew he'd never let anything or anyone hurt me if I was under his protection.

"Yes, I trust you. More than I would anyone else."

"Okay. Then whatever it is that's making you hesitate, get the fuck over it."

And *there* was the Sean I understood and could deal with.

"I don't have a problem pretending to like dick, so you shouldn't have a problem pretending to like—"

"*A* dick?" I interrupted, thinking of Henri's nickname for Detective Dick here.

"Don't think I don't know what Boudreaux calls me behind my back."

"You've got to admit, it kind of fits."

"Hey, if I'm a dick it's because it helps get the job done. I work with criminals most of the time, and asking nicely isn't always the best approach."

"Do you ever ask nicely for anything?"

Sean's lips quirked at the side. "Sometimes."

When he didn't elaborate, I decided my best bet was to let it go and move on. Sean was in an odd mood, and it was making my brain hurt. "So let's pretend I say yes to this asinine idea of yours. Then what?"

"Then I pack a bag and come home with you."

"Right now?"

"Well, I'm not about to let you walk out the door by yourself after what you told me, and I'm going to have to move in anyway."

As Sean's words lingered in the air between us, I knew he was expecting some kind of response, but I had nothing. The idea of Sean living with me was alarming.

"You said your boss wants a name by the morning—now you've got one. Let me pack a bag and we'll get going."

"Just like that?"

"Yeah, just like that."

"You don't have to tell anyone you're going? Or what you're doing?"

Sean looked around his empty living room. "You see anyone here?"

No. No, I did not. In fact, there was next to nothing here —people or possessions.

"I'd already put in for some leave at work, so that's covered. Just give me a few to pack and I'll be right out."

I knew I should tell him no. That this was a horrible idea. But Sean was already brushing by me and heading down the hall. It seemed my fate was sealed. I'd come in search of someone to guard my body, and ended up with the last person I'd ever expected.

6

SEAN

AROUND TWENTY MINUTES later, my duffel bag was packed, my house secured, and a less-than-enthusiastic Xander was pulling his sleek cobalt-blue Maserati convertible into my garage.

Since I'd be driving him to and from his destinations until we caught the lowlife who was threatening him, I figured it might be smart to take away one of the things his stalker friend would be familiar with.

Instead, we'd be utilizing my SUV. It was a deflection that wouldn't last long if this psycho was truly watching Xander's movements, but at least it would trip him up a little. The windows were tinted, it was in no way connected to Xander, and, as far as I was concerned, it was bigger, bulkier, and more likely to flatten someone than his fancy Italian sports car.

Xander grumbled as he climbed out and shut the door,

engaging the car alarm. "You're sure that your garage is secure?"

I crossed my arms and leaned against my SUV as Xander walked down the drive toward me. "No one's stolen my car yet."

Xander glanced past my shoulder, raised a brow, and then brought his eyes back to mine. "No offense, but an SUV is an SUV. This," he said, turning to gesture to the car he'd all but kissed goodbye. "This baby has a Ferrari-built 4.7-liter V8 engine. It goes from zero to sixty in four point five seconds."

"You're a car snob. Who knew."

"I'm not a snob. I just want to make sure it will still be here after all of this."

I pushed off the back of my SUV and walked over to him. "I'm more concerned with *you* still being here after all of this. But as for your precious car in there, I have security cameras on my property, and a couple placed at the entry points. One happens to be in the garage. You can check on your baby every night. Now let's go."

I hit the garage door remote, and as the door rolled down and Xander took one final look at his pride and joy, I climbed inside my car.

Not a minute later, the passenger door opened and Xander pulled himself up into the seat. As the interior light faded, he said, "Do you really think this person wants to hurt me?"

I didn't want to scare him, but I also didn't want to lie. "I don't know yet. But anytime someone gets this personal, when they become fixated on someone enough to send threats like this, you have to take it seriously."

Xander nodded, but stayed uncharacteristically quiet as he stared out the windshield.

"Are you scared?"

Xander shifted in his seat so he was facing me. "I'm more angry, if that makes sense. I thought I was going to have a nice, quiet night, and instead I've had to turn my life —and yours—upside down because some lunatic has a thing for me. That pisses me off."

"I get it. I'd be pissed too."

I started the engine, and Xander reached for his seatbelt and clicked it in place. "I just don't know how we're going to pull this off."

"Would you stop worrying about that? We'll work it out."

"And if we can't? Then what?"

I pulled out of the drive. "If for some reason we can't manage to fake it—"

"Which, you have to admit, seems likely to happen."

So much faith. "*If* that happens, I'll point you in someone else's direction."

Xander frowned. "I thought you said you were the best."

"I am."

"Then why would I want someone else?"

"My point exactly." I smirked. "Just keep that mindset and we should be golden. If you can have me, why would you *ever* want anyone else?"

Xander shook his head.

"I'm heading downtown, I assume?"

"Yes. North Lake Shore Drive. How weird is it that we've never been to each other's house until tonight?"

I shrugged and flicked on my indicator. "Never really had a reason before. We always have family dinners at Bailey's, and other than that, you and I never really—"

"If you say 'got along,' I'm going to kill you, since your whole argument that we could *pretend* to date is that we know each other so well."

I chuckled. "Calm down over there, Jesus. I was just going to *say* that you and I have never really had a reason to go to each other's house."

"I wish this wasn't the first."

"Yeah. Me too."

We fell silent, taking a moment to think about the way the night had unfolded. If someone had told me I'd be driving downtown to move in with Alexander Thorne and play his pretend boyfriend, I would've told them they had lost their mind. But the more I thought about the threats, the angrier I became, and the idea of letting someone else take care of this just didn't sit right.

For one, Xander was practically family, and us Baileys looked after one another. And two, if anything happened to the man sitting to my right, my brother would kill me. So the way I saw it, there was really no choice.

I knew Xander doubted my ability to pull this off, and if I thought about it too hard, I might agree. But if the alternative was him getting hurt—or worse—then I'd do everything in my power to make sure he was safe.

"Do you think we should call Bailey?"

I looked over to see Xander's phone in his hand and shook my head.

"Not yet. The less people who know, the better, for now. But we'll have to tell him eventually. Just in case a photo is leaked or—"

"A photo?"

"Well, you are famous, Xander. I've seen you on those entertainment shows, and I'm sure you're in magazines occasionally. What if Bay sees a photo of us together?"

"So what if he does? Maybe we ran into each other downtown."

"And just so happened to be holding hands?" Xander's mouth fell open, and when no words came out, I added, "That is what you said would need to happen to make this believable, right?"

Xander cleared his throat. "Yes. That's one of them."

"So yeah, we definitely need to let Bay know at some point. I'd hate having to explain *that* to him. What a shitshow."

Xander grimaced.

"So, you gonna tell me where I'm going, or what? I hate driving in the city."

"Why doesn't that surprise me?"

"Because you *know* me." I flashed a grin Xander's way. "I told you. This is going to be a breeze."

7

XANDER

"THIS IS ME." As the elevator glided to a stop at the twenty-fifth floor, Sean side-eyed me.

"Yeah, I kinda got that, since it's private and there's nothing else above us."

The last few minutes were the quietest Sean had been the entire way over here. After we'd parked, he'd insisted we stop by the lobby so he could take a quick look around before we went up to my place. But as the doors slid open and he stepped out into the narrow entrance hall, Sean stopped dead in his tracks and let out a low whistle.

Directly in front of him was a large marble feature wall with a beautiful gas-lit fireplace in the center. To the right, a slim feature window that rose from the floor to ceiling over-looked the city, and to the left was the way into the heart of the place.

I was about to step out and give him the guided tour,

when I heard, "Are you fucking kidding me with this place? *This* is where you live?"

Sean glanced over his shoulder at me, and as I walked out of the elevator and the doors slid shut, he shook his head.

"It's like a goddamn hotel." He paused for a moment and then added, "Not one that *I've* ever stayed in, but you know, one those classy fucking places."

As I moved around him, I took in the immaculate décor of the entry foyer and nodded. "I suppose I could see that."

Sean scoffed. "You suppose you could see—" He stopped in the foyer and looked from left to right. This was where the condo really showed its size, because you could choose to go either way, the apartment encompassing the entire twenty-fifth floor.

To the right were the bedrooms, pool, and gym, to the left the living areas, and the double doors directly in front of him opened up onto the terrace that surrounded the top floor of the building.

When it was clear Sean was at a loss for words, I turned to head toward the living room and kitchen.

"If you'll come with me, I'll make us both a drink and then show you around."

With his hand still gripping his duffel like it was a life-line back to a world he understood, I gestured toward it and said, "You can leave that here if you like."

Sean looked down to his bag and nodded. "Yeah, uh, okay." He placed it on the floor by one of the cream accent chairs and began to follow me through the halls.

As we passed by one of the many seating areas, I looked

back to see him walking carefully as though he was inside a museum, and I couldn't help but grin.

He was usually so confident and sure of himself, and I'd never seen Sean look so out of place, so...uneasy because of his surroundings. He reminded me of a bull in a china shop, or a little kid who'd been told to keep his hands to himself and not break anything. It was really rather endearing—until, of course, he opened his mouth.

"Fucking hell, Xander. I was joking around about the fancy ass skyrise. But this place is a little over the top, don't you think? I mean, you're the only one who lives here. How many bedrooms does a person need?"

I stopped at the entrance to my kitchen and turned to him. "About ten more if it puts distance between you and me."

"Hilarious."

I flashed him a fake grin as I made my way to the fridge and opened the door. I looked at the fully stocked shelves. "What's your poison tonight? Beer, wine, something harder?"

When I got no response, I looked over my shoulder and saw Sean walking around the kitchen island and heading toward the main feature of the place—the great room.

With a soaring twelve-foot dome ceiling that housed an elaborate chandelier, the rotunda sitting area offered mesmerizing views of both the city and the lake from every vantage point.

A luxurious leather couch curved around each side for maximum viewing potential, and when Sean came to a stop on the plush white rug, he placed his hands on his hips and slowly pivoted, taking in the multitude of twinkling lights outside the floor-to-ceiling windows.

"Ho*ly* shit."

I shut the fridge door and braced myself for whatever smartass comment he was about to make. But when nothing came, and Sean just stood there looking out at the million-dollar view surrounding him, I waited in silence, letting him drink it all in.

"I...I didn't even know places like this existed." He turned, and when he spotted me over in the kitchen, I smirked.

"They don't. I paid top dollar to make this one of a kind."

"One of a— This is a goddamn castle, Xander." Sean looked to the chandelier and dome ceiling above him. "You have a fucking turret."

A bark of laughter escaped me before I could rein it in, but Sean's reaction was priceless. He was so blue collar, even when he wasn't wearing a uniform. All of the Baileys were. They grew up with that "one of the boys" mentality. He loved his barbecues on the weekend, watching sports, and drinking beers in the afternoon.

I was the exact opposite. "It's not a turret. It's a rotunda."

"A what?"

"A ro— Oh, forget it." I headed in his direction, then stopped by a touchscreen control panel on the wall. "When I moved in and saw this view, I knew it would be a shame not to experience it from all angles. So I hired someone to make it...special."

"Uh, yeah, I'm pretty sure *special* might be a fucking understatement."

"I'm glad you think so. But not only does it provide views from wherever you stand, when you're sitting, and you press this button here"—I lightly brushed my finger over the controls, and Sean's eyes immediately fell to the floor moving under his feet—"the center of the room rotates."

Ahh... If only I could capture and replay this moment for Bailey and Kieran, because Sean completely and utterly gobsmacked was a rare occurrence. He looked like Alice after she'd fallen down the rabbit hole, and it was extremely gratifying to have tripped him up.

"Your fucking *floor* moves?"

"It does. It's a slow rotation, obviously," I said, as though there was nothing at all unusual about having a revolving living room. "Barely noticeable, except your view continues to change. It does a full 360 rotation in forty-five minutes."

The sheer bewilderment in Sean's eyes made me chuckle. It was the first time I'd felt like myself all night, and I could've hugged him for it. But I didn't, of course.

I turned on my heel and made my way back to the kitchen. "Ready for that drink now?"

8

SEAN

HOLY FUCKING SHIT.

Okay, Bailey had always said that Xander's place was unreal, like something out of a movie. But as I stood on his revolving living room floor, I didn't even think Hollywood could come up with this shit—only Xander.

Ever since I'd stepped off his elevator and into his palatial paradise, I realized that even though I'd known Xander for most of his life, I really didn't know anything about him at all.

For example, just how extravagant he was. From his car, to his clothes, to his fucking furniture, there was nothing subtle with this guy. Everything was designer or top dollar. Not that I cared. Xander could do whatever the hell he wanted with his money—God knew he had truckloads of it —but I couldn't wrap my head around the fact that the scrawny little kid that grew up next door to us, and still trekked out to the burbs for a barbecue every weekend, was the same guy who lived in this modern-day castle.

It was baffling.

"So? Your poison?" Xander asked for the second time tonight. "Beer? Wine?"

"A water's fine, thanks." His place had already made my head spin, so the last thing I needed was alcohol. Plus, I'd been steering clear of the stuff for the past few months and, I had to admit, felt better for it.

"Water it is." Xander pulled a glass carafe out of the fridge and placed it on the kitchen counter before grabbing two glasses from one of his pristine white cabinets.

The place was immaculate, with clean lines and nothing out of order. But then again, he probably had a maid. I couldn't imagine Xander carving out a day for cleaning, especially a place this massive.

"So...how are we going to do this?" Xander said, pushing a glass across the counter as I made my way out of the turret thingy and into his kitchen.

"Well, from the looks of it, I'm assuming this place is monitored by security cameras. In the garage, the lobby—what about the elevator? Do you know if they have any in there?"

Xander took a sip of water. "I sure hope not."

His tone made it pretty obvious what he was getting at, and not wanting to linger on the idea of him having sex in the elevator I just rode up in, I chose to ignore him.

"I'll check that out in further detail later. Do you know the building manager's name?"

"Yes, it's Gerald."

"Good. I'll fill him in on what's going on and make sure access to your floor is restricted. But I want to make sure his staff is kept in the dark as far as who I am. They will know me as your boyfriend. Only he will know me as more. Work for you?"

"Do I really have a choice?"

"No."

"Then it works for me."

"Thought it might. For now, though, what we're really going to have to focus on is your comings and goings. Where do you go after work, before work, for lunch? Do you have any habits? The gym? The coffee shop you go to every morning? I'll also want to check out your workplace, the people around you, but we can start on that tomorrow."

Xander set his glass on the counter and brushed a hand through his hair, the thick strands falling back in the exact position they'd been styled in that evening for his broadcast —always camera ready.

"This is crazy. I still can't believe it's actually happening. That you have to be here, dealing with this."

"Better me than some stranger, no?"

"I suppose."

"Gee, thanks."

"I didn't mean that."

"Yeah, you did, but I don't care. You need help, Xander, so suck it up and deal with it."

Xander's eyes flared at my no-nonsense tone, and he crossed his arms. "Fine. I'll deal with it. I'll even deal with you if it means staying alive. But this is all going to be for nothing if we can't make it believable."

"The cover story, you mean? You're still hung up on that?"

"Yes. You're saying you need to be with me around the clock, and I understand that the best way to do that is to have people think we're dating, but—"

"But what?"

Xander looked me over and shrugged. "I would never date someone who dresses as badly as you. Not to mention the way you act and talk. I just—I guess I don't understand how we're going to convince people this is real."

Not offended in the slightest by Xander's assessment of the things he found lacking in me, I placed my hands on the counter and gave him a once-over.

"News flash, Mr. Anchorman. I would never date someone like you either. You know, since you have a cock."

Xander arched an eyebrow. "See, this is exactly what I'm talking about."

"Oh, come on. It's called undercover for a reason. We act. It's not like I'm a pimp or some druggie living on the streets, but I seemed to play a pretty convincing role there. I just need to do a little background, a little research about the kind of guys you date to get into my role."

"So basically you're going to ask me a bunch of personal, invasive questions."

"You catch on quick."

"Lucky me." His droll tone made me laugh.

"It's not going to be that bad."

"Says the man who *won't* have to answer intimate, personal questions to someone he grew up with."

"Are you feeling shy? That doesn't seem like you."

He shot a death glare my way. "How about murderous?"

"Probably not the best choice, all things considered." And just like that, the mood in the room shifted back to serious, as we both remembered why I was there in the first place.

"So." I cleared my throat. "I'm going to need names of your past flings, hookups, whatever, and I'm going to ask you some questions about them. You need to answer me honestly."

"Wonderful."

I fished out the small notepad I kept in the back pocket of my jeans. "You got a pen?"

Xander looked to the small pad. "You just keep one of those in your back pocket?"

I shrugged. "Habit, I guess."

"Wouldn't it make sense to carry a pen too?"

Well, yeah, I supposed it would, but—"Do you have a pen or not?"

Xander walked to the opposite end of the counter, opened a draw, and pulled out a pen and an A4-sized notepad. I went to take it. But when he didn't immediately let go, I aimed a questioning look his way.

"Whatever I tell you here," he said, "it stays between us."

"As opposed to..."

"What do you think?"

"Ahh...you got some secrets rattling around this castle, Xander?"

Xander narrowed his eyes. "I just want to make sure that my private life stays *my* private life."

I tugged on the pen and paper, and when he let it go, I smirked. "Who am I going to tell?"

"I mean it. Not even Bailey, okay?"

I eyed him for a beat, and when Xander didn't waver I gave a clipped nod, wondering what exactly he was being so protective of. I figured Bailey would know anything and everything, them being best friends and all—but maybe not.

"Understood. What's this for?" I said, holding up the pad.

"You're going to need more paper than that tiny notebook if you want to know all of my hookups since Bailey. I like to have sex—often. It's a good release from a stressful job. When I have downtime, I make sure to find it. I also make them sign an NDA, so I have all their information for your background checks. You can use *that* to write down any traits I find attractive, other than the fact they have a cock. Which is the only requirement I'm looking for, according to you."

As Xander held my stare, I made sure not to react. He was pushing, waiting for me to tell him I was out, that this was too weird or uncomfortable. But as I stood there in his mammoth kitchen in a silent standoff, all I could think was how interesting his eyes were.

Really, they were, like, turquoise or some shit.

"Earth to Sean?" Xander waved his hand between us. "Did you hear me?"

"Oh, uh, yeah. Basically you like to fuck. So do most guys. That's nothing new."

"Wow." Xander pinched the bridge of his nose. "How you don't have a girlfriend is such a mystery."

"Who said I want a girlfriend?" When Xander dropped his hand and looked at me, I added, "My job doesn't really make dating easy. Guess I'm kinda like you in that sense. Casual hookups work better. That way I don't have anyone nagging me about my long hours, the danger associated with it, blah blah blah."

"Don't you get lonely?"

"Don't you?" I shook my head. "I like my space. Haven't really found anyone I want to share it with yet."

"Or anyone that *would*."

"Hey, I don't see anyone else living here." I looked around the enormous kitchen. "So I'd be careful on passing judgment."

Xander picked up our glasses and placed them in the sink, and after he put the carafe back in the fridge, he gestured with a tilt of his chin for me to follow him.

As he took us back through the hall we'd entered through, I picked up my duffel and continued in the direction he was walking. We passed by an indoor pool and gym area that looked better equipped than the one I was a member at. Then we continued on past several bedrooms, all enormous, all fully furnished, until we finally came to the end of the hallway, where Xander stopped in front of a set of double doors.

"This is my room."

I glanced by his shoulder and nodded. "Okay, let's go."

"Excuse me?"

His look of disbelief made me snort. "I need to see your room, Xander. Don't worry, I don't want to sleep in it."

"Trust me, I wasn't worried. *You're* sleeping in there," he said, pointing to the room behind me.

"Works for me. Doesn't change anything, though. I still need to see it." I reached around him for the handles, and as I pushed the doors open and stepped inside, my jaw nearly fell open. Marble floors. If I'd thought the rest of the house was over the top, it had nothing on Xander's bedroom.

With the room situated at the far end of the building, the architect had used the corner angle and views to his advantage, that was for damn sure.

The second you stepped inside, you were greeted with one spectacular view after another, starting with the wall directly in front of you which was nothing but glass and showcased Lake Michigan. To the right of that was a half wall of windows that overlooked the sparkling lights of downtown Chicago.

But before you could even begin to appreciate that view, your attention was brought back inside, because the rest of that wall was made up of the wide backboard to the enormous two-tiered platform that housed Xander's bed, and it looked more like a stage than a place a person slept.

There was a fireplace opposite the bed, and a leather

settee in the corner of the room—you know, in case you couldn't find somewhere to sit in the other ten million rooms.

It was extravagant, opulent, a room that screamed decadence and sex. As I ran my eyes over the plush covers and satin cream sheets, I imagined how it would feel to slide between them, and my dick kicked in immediate response.

Wait...what the fuck?

When I realized I'd probably been standing there a little too long without speaking, I swallowed and reminded myself who this bedroom belonged to and that getting hard in here would send all the wrong kinds of messages.

So I looked over my shoulder to see Xander with his hands shoved in his pockets and did what I did best—I deflected.

"What? No spinning bed? Have to say, I'm a little disappointed."

9

XANDER

FIVE A.M IS an ungodly hour for most, but for me it's the vital hour. It's six in New York and the world is waking up. Anything and everything that broke in the handful of hours I'd been asleep was just starting to roll out over the news waves, and that was where my day began.

As I sat up and cracked my neck from side to side, I stared out at the glittering city below and wondered what the day would bring. In my line of work it could be anything from the mundane to breaking news, but my job was never boring.

After a much-needed shower, I toweled off, grabbed my black terrycloth robe, and then slipped into my Uggs before making my way back to my bedroom, where I picked up my phone and scrolled through my emails.

When there was nothing there of immediate importance, I dropped it in my pocket and headed across the room, more than ready to hunt down my first hit of caffeine.

I pulled open the double doors and clutched at my chest as my eyes locked on Sean, who had just stepped out in front of me.

I'd completely forgotten he was there, or purposely pushed it aside, but as my memory kicked back in, I said, "Did you sleep out here all night?"

"No."

When he didn't further elaborate, I took in his navy sweatpants, tight white t-shirt, and disheveled hair. His jaw was lined with dark stubble, and he looked half-asleep.

"Then what are you doing?"

"I heard your shower, so here I am."

I looked at him as though he'd lost his mind. "What do you mean, so here you are? I just walked out of my bedroom. Did you think something was going to happen to me?"

Sean's jaw bunched as he crossed his arms over his chest—a well-built chest, I couldn't help but notice. "I'm just making sure you're okay. That is why I'm here, isn't it?"

"I suppose it is. I just didn't realize you'd be so...diligent that you'd want to make sure I emerged from my bedroom intact."

Sean's eyes narrowed. "Yeah, well, maybe tomorrow I *won't* be so diligent. Who the fuck gets up at five in the morning, anyway?"

I pulled the bedroom door shut behind me and shrugged. "I do. Would you like to come and sweep the kitchen before I make my coffee? You never know who might be hiding in one of my cabinets."

I shook my head as I went to brush by him, but Sean reached out and grabbed hold of my upper arm.

"Do you think this is some kind of fucking joke?"

No, I didn't. But I'd always felt safe in my house, and I'd be damned if I let that creep change that now.

"You'd be wise to start taking this shit seriously, Xander. Some crazy fucker wants to get close to you. Do you understand that?"

Sean's eyes were fixed on mine, the seriousness of his words reminding me of everything that had happened after last night's show. "Yes, I do."

"Good. Then act like it." Sean let me go. "Don't underestimate this guy. Just because you live in a castle, doesn't mean it can't be breached."

I gave a clipped nod, and as Sean disappeared inside his room, he called out, "I take my coffee with cream and two sugars. I'll be out in a minute, then we'll settle in and work on this *list* of yours."

Nearly forty-five minutes later, I found myself looking at the clock in the living room and wondering if time had somehow stopped.

"*Okaaay,*" Sean drawled as he flipped several pages of his notepad back in place and tapped his pen on the top page. "I'm pretty sure we have a name here for each letter of the alphabet. So if you could let me know what the next name starts with, I'll try to keep them in some kind of order."

"You're having a really great time with this, aren't you?"

"By this, do you mean writing down your many, *many*

fuck buddies? Because no. I'm actually getting a hand cramp."

It was right in that moment that I wondered if killing Sean would be worth the life sentence I would get. Maybe the judge would be lenient if I relayed what a gigantic pain in the ass he was.

"I hate you."

"That's so sweet," Sean said, tossing the pad on the couch beside him. "And I'm touched that I'm the one man in Chicago that you don't want to—"

"Finish that sentence and I'm going to kick you in the balls."

Sean snorted. "I mean, they're pretty big and all, but I doubt even you could reach them from over there."

Choosing to ignore his dumb ass, I looked out the window. "I told you there was a lot."

"You didn't tell me there was enough to fill Madison Square Garden."

I cut my eyes to him lounging back in his seat with his legs kicked out, his arm resting along the back of the couch. "And I suppose you're a monk?"

"Hey, I can still count mine on both hands. Twice over, maybe, but at least I can. Can't say the same for you, Mr. *Playerrr*..." Sean smirked. "Gotta say, I didn't know you had it in you."

One of the reasons I tried to avoid being around Sean on my own was that way I had some hope of reining in my impulse to say something I would regret—case in point, "Who said 'in me' is the way I like it?"

Sean's forehead creased as though he were thinking that over.

"Ugh, forget it," I said, getting to my feet. "Are we done with this portion of the interrogation?"

"Yeah, I guess. But you might as well sit back down. We're not done with the rest of it."

"The *rest* of it? What else could you possibly need to know?"

"Let's see..." Sean picked up the pad. "What these guys look like. What kind of clothes they wear. How do they act when they're with you?"

"That's easy enough," I said, and planted my hands on my hips. "They look nothing like you, wear the complete opposite of anything you have in your wardrobe, and they act like they have a brain in their head."

Sean looked me over and then stood, and something in the way he was inspecting me made me back up a step.

"So, basically, you like to date yourself."

"Excuse me?"

"Well, the opposite of me would be you. No wonder you and Bailey didn't work. You were too busy searching for yourself."

Beyond irritated now, I glared at Sean's smug face. Jesus, he was being an ass this morning, and the more he pushed, the more worked up I got. Like that last comment. I knew he didn't mean it the way I took it, but he was a little too close to the truth.

Searching for myself? That was a pretty accurate description of how I'd felt during my relationship with

Bailey, and about halfway into it, I'd realized I wasn't going to find any answers with my best friend. It had been too comfortable, too familiar, and I already knew that version of myself. It was all the other parts, the hunger, the darker urges, the unexplainable restlessness within me that I didn't understand—and still didn't.

"Bailey is nothing like you," I said, more annoyed than I could remember being in a long time. "He has more compassion and feeling in his little finger than you have in your entire body. Maybe if you had more, people wouldn't actively avoid you."

As my words echoed off the twelve-foot ceiling, Sean's spine seemed to stiffen, and I took perverse satisfaction in knowing I'd finally landed a blow.

"Trust me," he said in a quiet voice I'd never heard before. "You're not the first to point it out. Our father drilled that into my head every day of my life."

Sean took a step away from me, and my gut twisted with guilt. "Sean—"

"We're done here." Sean's tone was as cold as an arctic blast. It froze me in place. "Let me know when you're ready to go to work."

I opened my mouth—to say what I had no clue—but it didn't matter anyway. Sean was already walking out of the room, which was probably for the best. Any longer in each other's company, and the likelihood we'd come out alive on the other side was slim to none.

. . .

SEVERAL HOURS LATER, I was climbing inside Sean's SUV, and the tense silence between us was the same as it had been earlier.

I couldn't believe this was happening. I'd just spent the morning having one of the most uncomfortable conversations of my life, only to wind up in a verbal sparring match that had ended with the two of us nearly killing each other.

I chanced a quick look in Sean's direction as he pulled out of the parking garage. This was not good. Sean had always been the king of inane conversation, so as he sat in broody silence, I found myself growing uneasier and uneasier. Because how in the world were we going to pull off this ridiculous charade if he wouldn't even talk to me?

"Do you know where the building is?" I asked, trying to get us back to some kind of normalcy.

"Yep, I Googled it."

"Okay." We sat there for a few more seconds, and when the silence started to border on uncomfortable, I said, "When we get there, I'll take you up to meet Marcus—"

"Marcus?"

"Marcus St. James. He's the president of the news division at ENN. My boss."

Sean tapped his fingers on the steering wheel. "And just how close are you and your boss?"

I frowned.

"Just making sure he shouldn't be on your list."

"Marcus? Definitely not. He's just my boss."

Sean gave me the side eye, and I could tell he didn't believe me.

"What?"

"Are you lying?"

I arched an eyebrow. "Why would I lie?"

"I don't know. 'Cause he's your boss."

"So?"

"That would be a sticky situation."

"I *highly* doubt it," I said, and when Sean just stared at me, clearly not understanding my joke, I sighed. "Trust me, he's the last person I'd ever date."

"Just making sure I've covered all my bases."

I rolled my eyes, wondering how I was going to get through the next eight hours, and muttered, "Yes. God forbid I have any dignity left by the end of this."

The rest of the trip we made in silence, and that seemed much more preferable than another verbal go-around with Sean Bailey.

10

SEAN

FOR THE THIRD time in the last twenty-four hours, I found myself standing shoulder to shoulder with Xander inside an elevator, wondering what the hell I was doing there.

I mean, I knew why I was there, but after our blow-up this morning, fuck if I knew why I'd stayed. I'd told myself several times over to just call one of the agencies I'd worked with before, hand off the case, and let this be done with.

Yeah, I was the best option for this, but right now Xander's life was more in danger from us coming to blows than any pervert tracking him.

This morning had been rough. That was my fault. I'd been pushing Xander, fucking around with him. But instead of brushing me off and walking away like usual, Xander had fired back. And damn, his aim had been spot-on.

Nothing pushed my buttons more than being compared to my brothers. Not because I didn't think they were stand-up guys—they were two of the best men I knew—but because we'd been pitted against each other our whole lives by a strict father who had aspirations that we follow in his footsteps. Especially his eldest boy.

Fuck, usually I kept that kind of shit to myself. But Xander had gotten under my skin with that jab about not measuring up to Bailey, and now he probably thought I was harboring secret jealous tendencies, which couldn't be farther from the truth.

I looked at him from out of the corner of my eye to see him scrolling through his phone. He hadn't said anything since our discussion about his boss, and I had a feeling I'd pissed him off again.

Well, what else was new? It wasn't like it was a stretch. Lots of people hooked up with their bosses, and it would've been shortsighted not to ask. I didn't see why he was so bent out of shape. Either way, I figured he'd get over it. That was how it always worked with us. I usually did or said something to annoy him, he'd get surly for an hour or so, and then we'd move past it.

It was like a well-rehearsed show we put on whenever we were near one another, which meant the next however many days were going to be a hard sell if we didn't pull our heads out of our asses, and soon.

"What are you looking at?"

I almost lied and said I wasn't looking at anything. But that wasn't my way, so I turned toward him and said exactly what was on my mind. A trait that usually landed me on a person's shit list. "I was just wondering how long you're going to be pissed off at me."

Xander's eyes narrowed and his expression turned murderous as he lowered his phone and pivoted so we were face to face.

"Me, mad at you? You're the one who's been ignoring me for the last however many hours. Don't start with me."

I could all but see the steam pouring out of his ears, as he no doubt tried to control his urge to lash out at me. Something I would've paid good money to witness, considering how immaculately put together he looked.

In designer jeans, a black button-up shirt, with his hair styled and his jaw clean-shaven, there was nothing out of place about him. Hell, I would've even laid bets his briefs were ironed.

"Don't start wh—"

"You know *exactly* what I'm talking about." Xander took a step closer to me. "You, poking at me. Trying to get a rise out of me. We're about to meet with my boss and coworkers, and I'd rather do that without thoughts of bloody murder on my mind."

"Hmm, confessing murderous intentions to a detective. And here I always thought you were smart."

Xander sighed. "Can we just call a truce now? Please? This is us."

As the elevator doors parted and we stepped out into the lobby, my eyes landed on a wall-sized poster of the man standing to my left, and my jaw nearly hit the floor.

Global News with Alexander Thorne was splashed

across the enormous promo poster. But what really caught and held my attention was the striking color of Xander's eyes in the image, in contrast to his hair.

That had to be photoshopped. Or maybe that was why he colored his hair that gunmetal color, to make his eyes pop.

I glanced over my shoulder to see for myself. "Do you color your hair?"

The appalled look on his face told me that was a definite no. I took a step toward him to get a closer look, but Xander held his hand up. "What the hell are you doing?"

"I'm looking to see if you're lying about your hair."

"And you think you can tell that by what, getting all up in my face?" Xander screwed his nose up. "You're an idiot."

"And you didn't answer my question."

"I don't plan to, either. It was rude, but that's nothing unusual for you. Let's go. Marcus is waiting."

Xander started off down a long hall. I caught up to him and slipped my hands into my pockets, then I had a thought. "Do you think we should practice holding hands now?"

Xander's head whipped around so fast that I was surprised he didn't break his neck. "Quit it, Sean."

"Quit what?"

"I don't know, just...quit it."

When Xander aimed a frosty glare my way, I couldn't help my broad smile. Finally, we were back to our usual selves.

"Hey, I'm just trying to get into the groove. And at least you're not thinking about the real reason I'm here now, are you?"

"No. I'm just wishing you were anywhere else."

I chuckled as we stopped in front of a large desk. A woman wearing thick, purple-rimmed glasses, glanced up and spotted us.

"Alexander." A cheerful grin that made her eyes twinkle lit up her face. "You can go straight in. He's expecting you."

"Thanks, Carmen." Xander said to me, "Try not to talk too much in there, would you? I find you're less offensive if you aren't speaking."

"Sure thing, *Alexander*."

Xander's eyes flared, and again I was captured by how unusual the shade was. Like the water around a tropical island. They just drew you in and made you want to linger there.

"Okay, so your hair might be real, but you definitely wear contacts, right?"

"What is wrong with you right now? My eyes have always been this color." The expression on his face relayed what a complete and utter moron he thought I was. "How long have you known me?"

Over thirty years, my brain instantly supplied.

"Let's go. Marcus doesn't like to be kept waiting."

I nodded and gestured for him to go first, and as he brushed past me, I heard myself say, "You can't blame me for asking. Your eyes are fucking... Wow. Can't believe I never noticed them before."

But then again, I'd never really had a reason to.

11

XANDER

YOUR EYES ARE fucking... Wow.

It had been nearly an hour, maybe more, since Sean had whispered that in my ear, and I was still trying to wrap my head around it. I couldn't decide if it had really happened, or if I was in such a weird headspace after the last twenty-four hours that I was imagining things. It sounded like Sean, but it was not like him to compliment me at all. Especially on something so...personal.

The meeting with Marcus had gone just as I expected. He'd done most of the talking, I'd barely said a word, and then Sean had explained his plan to come on board as my bodyguard in the role of my fake boyfriend.

I'd thought Marcus would nix that idea as ludicrous, but I was in for a shock. Instead, he'd given a brisk nod and then, thankfully, left for another meeting, because if Sean had had to go into detail on how exactly he was going to fill that role, I had no idea how I would've handled it with Marcus.

God, I needed to pull it together. Yes, this situation was weird, and yes, I'd rather not be in it. But wishing it would just disappear wasn't going to change the fact that someone was out there hunting me, and I needed protection. So the sooner I wrapped my head around things, the better.

After filling out a mountain of paperwork and HR issuing Sean an access badge—something Marcus felt he needed, to have access to the newsroom and my office at all times—we stepped out into the hall, where I caught sight of the clock and grimaced.

"You got somewhere you got to be?" Sean asked.

"Yes, actually. I had to miss tonight's first rundown so we could get this all cleared up, but—"

"Now you need to get up there. Gotcha. Let's go."

Sean started to walk off. I took hold of his arm and drew him to the side of the hallway. "Are you going come with me? Right now?"

"That is the reason I just signed my name on five thousand sheets of paper."

"Of course." I looked over his shoulder to the people busily working behind their desks, and then back to him. "So we have to start pretending to be..."

"Dating?"

I screwed my nose up, and Sean chuckled.

"You can't do that."

"What?"

"Look like you just swallowed something gross every time I say we're dating."

"Oh God. I can't do this. I'm not that good of an actor."

"Yeah, you can. I know this is like something out of bizarro world, but it's important. Your safety's at risk, and we need this—*us*—to be believable. So suck it up, buttercup."

I swallowed back my immediate impulse to argue. "You're right. You've been right ever since I knocked on your door. This is all just so...foreign."

"I know. But we've got this. Try to stop worrying."

Easier said than done. As we made our way down to the level the newsroom and my office were located on, the glass doors loomed up ahead. I looked over to Sean to gauge his mood, and when my eyes caught on his baseball cap, too-long hair, and his Chicago Bulls t-shirt, I groaned.

"Sean? Wait up a second, would you?"

He stopped, and I tried to imagine telling people we were dating with a straight face...and just couldn't.

"What?" When I stood there in silence, he let out a breath. "Xander?"

"Nothing. Sorry. I just wanted to make sure we're on the same page when we walk through those doors, that's all."

Sean glanced over his shoulder to where a flurry of activity could be seen beyond the glass.

"Ah, I see. Trying to work out how to explain us, huh?"

"Something like that," I said as my head began to throb with what would probably be a constant headache until all of this was over.

"Hmm." Sean crossed his arms. "What were you thinking? I'm your hot new lover who won't let you out of my sight?"

Definitely not. "No. I was thinking more that this is brand new and you wanted to come and see where I worked."

Sean shrugged. "What about Monday?"

"What *about* Monday?"

"Well, I'm going to be dropping you off and hanging around, so once *this* little tour is over, then what's my reason for being here?"

Yes, that headache wasn't going anywhere. "Maybe we'll get lucky and this will all be over by then."

Sean shook his head. "You need a better plan if that's what you're pinning all your hopes on."

"Okay, okay. On Monday, after you drop me off, I'll find a place for you to hang out. Somewhere private."

"Somewhere I can watch over you."

Though I knew that was why Sean was here, something about the way he said it made my pulse skip a few beats.

Not wanting to examine that too closely, though, I agreed. "Right. I'll talk to Marcus, and we'll have somewhere set up so you can see the broadcasting studio and the feeds for the newsroom."

"Your office, too. I need to be able to see in there. But yeah, that works."

Sean sidled up next to me then and slung his arm around my shoulders. As he tugged me into his side, I stumbled into him. The move was awkward and...well, weird, and when I glared at him, he grinned.

"You're gonna have to sell it better than that. The fact you find me irresistible."

Okay, I really needed to stop thinking of him as Sean—Bailey's annoying older brother—if there was any hope in hell of making people believe I was into him. I closed my eyes and channeled all of the drama classes I'd ever taken in high school. When I reopened my eyes, I aimed my most sensual smile in Sean's direction.

He chuckled, and then lowered his mouth by my ear. "Keep that up, Mr. Thorne, and I just might just start to believe you myself."

Shit, what the hell was that? Goosebumps covered my arms, as my entire body seemed to react to the way he'd just said "Mr. Thorne." *Jesus, Xander. Get it together.*

"You ready?"

No. "Yes. Let's get this over and done with."

"Great attitude."

"My attitude is the least of my concerns." My confused body was now number one. I took in a deep breath and then let it out. "Just...don't oversell it, okay? No one will believe it if you do."

"So you're saying I shouldn't make out with you on your desk right away?"

I groaned. "Sean..."

"I'm just fucking with you. Relax. This is gonna be a piece of cake."

He squeezed my shoulders, and I glared at him as he led us toward the doors. When he let me go to pull one open, I felt like I was stepping into the Twilight Zone.

"Oh good, you're here," Ryan said from across the room when he spotted me. "Jim is looking for you. Something about an update to the first run-through he wants you to look over before he approves. But he said he'll catch you in the final."

Completely ignoring Sean, Ryan continued on as though it was a normal day and I didn't have a gigantic shadow looming over my shoulder.

"Your suit is hanging in your office, but they left off the tie. I told them to get it over here ASAP, but they couldn't guarantee it would be here before you went on air. Stephanie is trying to track one down as we speak. But if worse comes to worse, I'm sure we can find someone around here wearing one we could use."

Ryan finally acknowledged Sean by giving him a once-over, but then shook his head. "Clearly not him."

"Got it," I said. "Thanks. Anything else?"

Ryan seemed to think about that for all of two seconds then shook his head. "Nope. Team's ready when you are for the final run-through, but everything else is good to go."

"Okay. Just give me a few minutes, and I'll be there." Then, because I could feel Sean boring a hole in the back of my head, I plastered a smile on my face.

"Sean, this is Ryan, my assistant." I looked to Ryan and repeated on a loop in my head, *Sell it. Sell this ridiculous lie and get it over with.* "Ryan, this is Sean. He's going to be sitting in on the broadcast tonight. A behind-the-scenes tour."

It didn't escape me—or Sean, judging by the coughing fit he suddenly came down with—that I'd purposely left out *who* Sean was. Guess I wasn't that great of a liar after all.

That was soon cleared up, however, when Ryan held his hand out and Sean shook it.

"Hi. So, um, are you going to be working here?"

"Ha." Sean laughed and put his hand on my shoulder. "Nope, that's all Xander. I just wanted to come and see where my boyfriend spends his nights when he's not at home with me."

Was he kidding? What part of "don't oversell it" did he not understand? He might as well have stamped PROPERTY OF SEAN'S on my forehead.

"Boyfriend, huh?" Ryan's eyes found mine and I schooled my expression, hoping it didn't scream, *Not in this lifetime*. I must've pulled it off, because he grinned and waggled his brows. "You never said anything about a boyfriend."

Think, Xander. Think. "I know. I was keeping things quiet until it got serious."

"Oh, a *serious* boyfriend."

Fuck.

Ryan grinned as he looked Sean over. "Well, I can see why you'd keep him a secret. I'd keep him to myself too until it was locked in."

Was Ryan actually checking Sean out? It was official: my life was getting more peculiar by the second.

"Well," Ryan said when he managed to drag his eyes away from Sean. "I know what the news is going to be about around here tonight, and it's nothing that's in the rundown."

Great. Just great. Sean chose that exact moment to take my hand in his, and it took everything I had not to jerk away.

How was he acting so natural, so normal under such *abnormal* circumstances?

"There's no news here," I said, my tone much more clipped than usual, as I started off toward my office, tugging Sean along behind me. "Just let everyone know we'll do the run-through in fifteen."

Ryan turned to watch us go, and somehow I knew that wouldn't be the only thing he'd let everyone know by the time he was done.

Oh well, Sean had wanted our cover story to get around. Wish granted. This gossip was about to spread through the station like wildfire. I just hoped he was ready to face the heat.

12

SEAN

"I THINK YOUR assistant likes me." I looked out the glass door of Xander's office to where Ryan kept glancing over his shoulder in our direction. "He keeps looking back here. Think I should wave?"

"I think you should sit down and stop making a spectacle of yourself."

The pissy tone with which Xander delivered that suggestion told me he wasn't impressed by my acting chops back there. But I thought I deserved an Oscar. It wasn't easy pushing past my automatic impulse to annoy the shit out of Xander. Not to mention touch him and hold his hand like it was an everyday occurrence.

I was trying here, but it was only going to work if he loosened up.

"No thanks. I'm fine standing. But you wanna maybe tell me what crawled up your ass between the HR department and now?"

Xander looked up from his computer and pinned me with what I was going to refer to as his *I wish the floor would open up and swallow you whole* look.

"Nothing *crawled* up my ass," he said as he slowly rose to his feet. "But maybe *you* could explain how announcing to my assistant that you are my boyfriend was not overselling things?"

"Well you weren't going to tell him."

"No, I was going to let him speculate."

"Speculate?" I walked over and stopped at Xander's desk. "We don't have time to let him speculate. We need this whole office buzzing over your new piece of man meat as soon as possible. And in case you missed the memo, that happens to be me."

Xander clenched his jaw and pressed all ten of his fingers into the top of his desk so hard that I thought he might break them.

"You are quite possibly the most annoying human being I have ever met. Did it ever occur to you that I might like to ease into things? I have to work with these people, and now they're all out there gossiping about me."

I crossed my arms and gave him a bored look. "And?"

"*And* I'm not the kind of guy who parades around his latest..."

When words seemed to escape him, I suggested, "Fuck?"

Xander's eyes blazed as he jabbed a finger at me. "Stop it."

"Stop what?"

"Acting like this should all be so fucking simple," Xander thundered, and his voice was so loud it all but blasted me out of his office. Seeming to realize that anyone on the floor could've heard the commotion, he took a deep breath and said in a much calmer tone, "My life was turned on its *ass* last night."

"I know."

"Do you?" Xander marched around the desk until we were standing toe to toe. His jaw was locked, his fists balled, and he looked more furious than I could ever remember seeing him. "You seem to be acting like this is all some big joke. Ha ha, I have to play Xander's boyfriend, no sweat. I'll hold his hand and tell everyone we're fucking, right? Well, this isn't some joke to me, Sean. This is my life."

I wasn't quite sure what to say. Of course I didn't see this as a joke, but I could see how he might have taken it that way.

"Xander—"

"Not now," he said, and held a hand up. "I have to go and sit in on the run-through and write up my script. Then I need to get ready to go on air." He took a step back and moved around me. "You're welcome to come with me, or stay in here. But if you step out of this door and back into my world, so help me, Sean, you *will* keep your mouth shut."

Deciding to concede this round to him, I nodded. Clearly I needed to rethink my approach.

"Good, I'm glad we understand one another." Xander pulled the door open and stormed out, and all I could think as I stared after him was that I didn't understand him at all.

But this was a great place to start.

THE WAR ROOM—THAT was where I found myself sitting not too long after our little blow-up, and I was one hundred percent convinced that I was the dumbest person in there.

Positioned in the back corner of the room, I had a good view of everyone as they went through the bullet points on the whiteboard, which, I quickly discovered, was how Xander worked out what he was going to report on when he went on air.

There were four segments, each known as a block, and as they went through each of the possible stories that could go in the A block, B block, and so on, Xander yea'd or nay'd them, rattling off reasons for each decision as he went along.

Not important enough for the top of the program.

Too important to be at the bottom.

Don't have enough sources to consider the story credible.

Can't get hold of a professional in time to confirm facts.

I mean, shit, who knew how much time went in behind the scenes to put on a thirty-minute news program? But the place was a hive of activity, not an idle hand in sight, as they all worked to figure out the order of things before Xander had to sit down at his desk and inform the country.

Speaking of Xander, he was seated about as far away from me as I figured he could possibly get, and everyone in the room was focused on him, waiting to see what he was going to approve or throw out.

Directly next to him was a frazzled guy, Jim—he was Xander's EP, whatever that was. He was definitely someone I wanted to know more about, though, since he seemed to be the one Xander listened to above everyone else.

"Okay," Jim said, and then pointed to something on the papers in front of Xander, who nodded. Then he looked at the rest of the group. "Does anyone have a problem with any of the stories on the board?" When no one spoke up, he said, "Good. You all have your assignments. Stephanie? Try to see if you can get someone on the phone that has any kind of expertise in child psychology. If you find someone, we'll somehow fit the story in around the A or B block."

"Got it," Stephanie, with the blonde ponytail, said.

"Good. Everyone else, we've got an hour until go time, and I don't want any fuck-ups."

As everyone got to their feet, Jim pointed to the guy sitting directly in front of me. Brent was an intern, someone had said earlier, and I wondered if his beard was as itchy as it made me feel looking at it.

"You're on the assignment desk," Jim said. "Anything comes in, you let me know. Got it?"

"Got it," Brent said, and then disappeared out the door.

When everyone had left except for Xander, Jim, and myself, I waited for my next cue from the man of the hour. I'd done as he'd asked and kept to myself while he worked, and I'd be damned if I stepped out of line now.

If Xander wanted me to play it cool, I could do that. Let him explain me.

"Hi there," Jim said as he headed in my direction. "I

didn't get a chance to introduce myself earlier. I'm Jim, Xander's EP."

I got to my feet and shook his hand. "I'm Sean. And I have no idea what an EP is."

"Most don't. But basically, I boss Xander around when he's on air, and he lets me."

"Nice to see how you view our relationship, Jim," Xander said.

Jim grinned. "Ignore him. He knows the truth. So, you're the boyfriend everyone's buzzing about, huh?"

I looked to Xander, who rolled his eyes, and decided there was no harm in confirming what was already out there. "That's right. I guess that makes me your new competition for his time, huh?"

"That sounds about right." Jim gave me a once-over I wasn't quite sure what to make of. "Well, it's nice to meet you, Sean."

As he headed out the door and I found myself alone with Xander again, I said, "What was that about?"

"What?" Xander asked, not bothering to look up from the papers in front of him.

"That look he just gave me."

As I stood on Xander's left, he put his pen down and finally looked up at me. "Probably disbelief."

"Disbelief?"

"Yes." Xander pushed back from his chair with his papers in hand. "Disbelief that I would date someone who dresses like you."

I glanced down at my shirt and jeans. "What's wrong with the way I'm dressed?"

"Nothing. But Jim knows me, and he's probably wondering when I started dating men like, well, you."

Xander brushed by me, and when he got to the door, he stopped and looked back. "I need to go and get ready to go on air. You can wait in my office, if you like."

Yeah, okay, that all sounded fine to me, but... "I still don't understand what's wrong with my clothes. What *should* I be wearing?"

My question was left unanswered, though, because Xander had already left the room.

13

XANDER

WHEN I STEPPED out of my bedroom the next morning to find Sean waiting on the other side of the door, I wasn't at all surprised. Although I'd prepared myself for his presence mentally, the reality of seeing him first thing in the morning wasn't something I could ever see myself getting used to.

Yesterday had been frustrating and humiliating, and I was ashamed to admit I had let my temper get the better of me several times over. I'd barely spoken to Sean after the broadcast, and when we arrived home, I'd excused myself and gone straight to my room.

This bodyguard thing was...unnatural. Having someone with you twenty-four seven was suffocating and made you conscious of every single move you made. Not to mention very aware of where that person was and what they were doing.

I'd never been more attuned to Sean in my life. Add in

the fact that my entire newsroom now believed we were dating, and I'd never felt more off balance either.

"Good morning, sunshine." The shit-eating grin that accompanied Sean's greeting made me sigh.

"Are you really this cheerful in the morning, or are you doing it to—"

"Annoy you?" Sean pushed off the wall and nodded. "You got it."

"Mission accomplished," I grumbled, as I walked by him and we headed toward the kitchen.

"So, last night was interesting," Sean said, and I quickly discovered that his version of interesting and mine varied greatly.

"Not sure that's how I'd describe it."

"No? Then how would you?"

I flicked on the kitchen light and turned to look at him barefoot in his grey sweats and a navy t-shirt with CPD and the police department emblem on the pocket.

"How about irritating, inconvenient, and humiliating." As I turned on my heel to head to the fridge, Sean took up a seat at the counter.

"Are we back to that again? I thought you would've simmered down after getting your beauty sleep."

My hand froze where it was on the handle, and I glared over my shoulder at the most infuriating man I'd ever met. "Simmered *down*? Do you even think about the stuff that comes out of your mouth before you say it?"

"What? It's an accurate description, isn't it? You were all riled up yesterday, and I just thought—"

"Stop thinking," I snapped, and then let go of the fridge to brace my hands on the counter. "In fact, stop talking. It's not even six yet, and I don't have enough caffeine in my system to deal with you."

"Oh, come on, Xander. When are you going to stop being pissed about all of this and realize I'm here to help you?"

I stared at him and felt my indignation leave me in a rush of air. I *was* angry, pissed off that some stranger had decided to zero in on me with his perverted fascination and in the process disrupted my day-to-day routine.

But it wasn't Sean's fault. He was doing me a favor. He'd just been the most convenient punching bag around, and, I was ashamed to admit, I'd taken advantage of that.

"You're right," I said. "I know you're right, and I'm sorry. I'm just so...so—"

"Angry?"

"Yes." I shrugged. "But there's nothing I can do about it but deal with it."

"Right. And that's what we're doing. You're not alone in this, you know."

"I know." I rubbed my hands over my face and then went back to the fridge. "Do you want a coffee?"

"Nah, I'm good. But maybe make yours a little stronger today."

I placed the milk on the counter. "Why's that?"

"Because in about twelve hours, we have to work out how to tell Bailey about all of this."

Shit. I looked at the clock, and sure enough, it was just

about to turn six. Great, how in the world was I going to explain all of this to Bailey when I couldn't even seem to wrap my own head around it? Maybe I should just leave it up to Sean. He seemed to be the most levelheaded about all of this, but then again, that was his job.

"I can tell him, if you like," Sean said as if reading my mind, and my gut instinct was to agree and let him deal with it. But either way, I knew Bailey would come to me once he found out.

"No. It needs to come from both of us."

Sean nodded. "Well, don't worry about it yet. I just wanted to put it out there."

Yeah, because it was as easy as that to just turn off the worry switch.

"How about we focus on something else for a second?" he asked.

"Like?"

"Like how interesting your job is. I've never been in a television studio before. I guess I didn't realize how much went into your day before you actually sat down in front of the camera."

I pushed the button on the coffee machine and leaned back against the counter. "What? You thought I rocked up thirty minutes before I went on air, recorded the news, and went home?"

"Well, yeah."

I chuckled and shook my head. "I'm the editor of my newscast. I have final say on all the stories, write all my scripts, and spend most mornings here poring over the news before I even go in at around eleven. It's a full-on job, one that requires ninety percent of my time, and I wouldn't change it for the world."

"I get that," Sean said as he leaned forward. "My job's much the same. Weird, long-ass hours. Hard to turn off when you leave the place. But worth it when you put some evil motherfucker behind bars."

Up until now, I'd never really thought I had that much in common with Sean, but I had to admit, our lives were more similar than I'd imagined.

"Do you ever think about leaving it?"

Sean was shaking his head before he even answered. "Nah, I don't know how to do anything else. And honestly, I'm pretty fucking good at it."

I laughed. "If you say so yourself."

"I do. Don't tell me you don't think you're good at your job."

I grabbed myself a coffee cup. "Oh, I know I'm good at my job. Do you see where I live?"

Sean scoffed. "Money isn't everything, you know."

"I know. But it sure is nice to have." I flashed a smile, and when his eyes lowered to my mouth, I felt a frisson of heat race through my veins.

No. No, no, body. That's Sean. You don't act like this with Sean. Get with the program.

"So, um, you said you put in for leave the other night," I said, trying to distract myself from whatever the hell that just was. "Did something happen or did you just need a break?"

Sean blinked and then refocused on my face, and his eyes held a confusion I decided to ignore.

"Uh, no. Nothing happened. I mean, we wrapped up a long case and I just realized I hadn't been around family much. I can't remember the last time I was at Saturday night dinner."

"Me either."

"Aww, did you miss me?"

My gut instinct was to say no, but I told the truth. "Your absence was noted."

"And celebrated?"

I frowned and wondered if Sean really thought we preferred those dinners when he wasn't there. "Why would you say that?"

Sean schooled his features and turned to look out at the view of the city. "Was just a joke."

That's what he wanted me to believe, but I knew better. "I hope so, because your brothers? They love you."

Sean turned back to face me, the pensive expression in his eyes unreadable, but then he blinked and it seemed to vanish, and in its place was a smile.

"They tell you that, or you just guessing?"

"Bailey told me. Kieran would rather die than admit he *has* feelings, so with him I'm just guessing."

"Seems about right. Speaking of Bailey, how is he?"

The coffee finished brewing, and I added some milk. "He's great. Henri's finally settled in, and the two of them seem really happy together. Do you want some juice, water, anything?"

"I'll take juice," Sean said, and after I poured it and grabbed my coffee, I came around the counter and took the seat beside him.

We sat there in silence for a moment, and I couldn't help but think how odd it was to be sitting with Sean in my kitchen before sunrise. Then he leaned in and bumped shoulders with me.

"Does it bother you?"

I took a sip of my coffee. "Does what bother me?"

"That it's not you he settled down with?"

The question was so out of the blue that it stumped me for a second. But after fully processing it, I shook my head. "No. I love Bailey, and I always will. But we worked out a long time ago we were better as friends."

Sean slowly nodded. "I figured. There's not too many people who can go back to best friends after...you know."

"Fucking?"

Sean screwed his nose up. "Uh, I'd rather not think about my brother doing anything remotely...naked."

I chuckled and took another sip of my coffee. "Fair enough."

Sean ran a hand though his hair, and when I spotted a hole in his t-shirt just under his ribs, I couldn't stop myself from sticking my finger in it.

"Your shirt has a hole in it."

Sean looked down at the rip and then shrugged. "One hole. And you can't even really see it when my arm's down."

"You can't even— Are you serious?"

"About my shirt? Yeah. I'll keep it until it spreads."

"No. No, no. There's no way I am dating—even *fake* dating—someone who wears shirts with holes in it." I then looked to his too-long hair and stubble. "You know what we're going to do today?"

"Sew up my shirt."

The idea of Sean with a needle and thread was so preposterous that I couldn't help but laugh. "No. I'm going to give you a makeover."

Sean's eyes widened as he jumped to his feet. "Uh-uh. Hell no. I've seen those makeover shows, and there's no way you are getting me in a pink shirt and tailored pants, all in the hope I'll get in touch with my inner fashion goddess."

"Okay. First off, I think you've been watching too many of those shows. Second, you couldn't pull off pink if you tried. Third, you are doing this because it will make me happy, and I've had a really shitty couple of days."

Sean looked to the ceiling and shook his head. But when he said, "You put me in anything pastel and I *will* shoot you," I felt better than I had in days.

14

SEAN

"I DON'T KNOW about this, Xander." I stared at myself in the full-length mirror of the dressing room Xander had shoved me into a few minutes ago and looked over the first outfit he'd picked out for me.

It was unlike anything I would've chosen for myself, and as I studied the fit of the tailored black pants, burgundy cable-knit shirt, and black sports coat, I felt like I was dressing for some upper-class dinner, not my day-to-day life.

Who dressed like this?

"Stop complaining," Xander said through the door. "I didn't give you anything that was too patterned or overly bright. I kept to the darker shades to match your winning personality. So get your ass out here and show me the first one."

This was ridiculous, and if someone asked me why I'd agreed to this plan, my only excuse was that Xander had caught me in a weak moment, before the sun came up.

I ran a hand through my long strands and again thought about how I needed to get it cut, then I turned and reached for the door handle.

As I went to unlock it, Xander called out, "Don't even think about coming out of there unless you have a different outfit on than you walked in with."

Damn, who knew Xander was such a bossy shit? "I have on a different outfit. Jesus, calm down already."

I pulled open the door, and like he'd been standing with his ear to it, Xander reared back. As he straightened and his eyes landed on me, they widened a fraction.

"See, I told you. I look ridiculous in this designer shit. Give me jeans and a t-shirt any day."

Xander held a hand up and took a step toward me. "You're wrong. This, this is..." He narrowed his eyes as he looked me over. "Where's the belt?"

"Huh?"

"The belt?" Xander brushed by me and stepped into the dressing room. When he came back out with a black leather belt, I screwed my nose up.

"I don't need that. The pants fit fine."

"It's not to hold them up, it's to finish off the look."

As he stepped in close to me and reached for the bottom of my shirt, his fingers brushed against the bare skin of my abdomen, and the unexpected touch created a spark of electricity that nearly made me jump away from him.

"What the hell are you doing?"

Xander frowned as though I was a moron, and consid-

ering he'd just told me what he was doing, I guessed that was
how I sounded.

"I was going to thread the belt. But here, tuck your shirt
in and put this on."

"Who tucks in a cable knit?"

"If it's lightweight, there's nothing wrong with tucking it
in." Xander cocked his head to the side. "And who here has
worked with designers and knows what he's talking about?"

Grumbling, I turned to face the mirror and did as I was
told. Once everything was in place, I let out a belabored
breath and turned back to face my "stylist."

"Well?" I said. "I was right, wasn't I? It looks better
without the belt."

"Stop talking."

I found myself doing as Xander said again, and as he
walked around behind me, I suddenly felt very self-
conscious about what he was thinking. Why, I had no
fucking idea.

"Wow."

I looked over my shoulder. "Wow, what?"

Xander didn't look annoyed, didn't look pissed off. He
looked—

"You should get this outfit."

—impressed.

As he walked back around to stand in front of me, I
stood a little taller under his inspection. I squared my shoulders and puffed out my chest. I figured if I could impress
Alexander Thorne—my biggest critic—then maybe this
outfit wasn't so bad after all.

"You like it, huh?"

"I just said you should get it, didn't I?"

"Yeah, but I'm asking you what you *think*. Like, if we didn't know each other, and I was walking down the street? Would this make you do a double take?"

"But I do know you."

"Yeah, but if you didn't." I wasn't sure why or what I was pushing for.

Xander pointed to the dressing room and said, "Would you get back in there? You have five other outfits to try on and this is just the first store," and I felt frustrated by his lack of response.

I headed back into the dressing room, and just as I went to shut the door, Xander said, "Sean?"

"Yeah?"

"If I didn't know you, there'd be no double take, just the one. That outfit makes it difficult to look anywhere else."

Well, what do you know. "You think I'm hot."

"And *that* is why I didn't answer."

"You totally think I'm hot in this...this fancy-schmancy getup."

"Uh-huh." Xander let out a bored sigh. "You're so hot, Sean. I'm not sure how I'm resisting you right now."

"Ha. Say what you want, but you already admitted it. You think I'm hot, and I think you're right. Maybe I should've had you and Bailey picking my clothes out for me all along."

"Oh God. Would you listen to yourself? Not all gay men are into shopping and designer clothes. In fact, your brother hates shopping. Please, be a little more obnoxious. It's reminding me of who you really are."

"Eh, you've always known who I am."

"And suddenly I'm wishing I didn't."

I flashed a toothy grin his way, and when Xander returned a scowl, I laughed and shut the dressing room door. I had five more outfits to go, and if Xander's response to the first was anything to go by, maybe this painful experience would be over much sooner than I'd anticipated.

All in all, this shopping thing wasn't so bad.

15

XANDER

AFTER ONE TOO many hours shopping with Sean, I decided I deserved an award for putting up with what had to be the most torturous experience of my life.

At first, I'd thought it would take my mind off things. If I was out and busy, maybe it would distract me from the real reason I had to hang out with him in the first place. But as Sean pocketed his wallet and grabbed his most recent purchase from the salesclerk, I was soon reminded why.

One minute, I was staring aimlessly out the wide windows of the store, watching the Saturday shoppers walking by and gathering at the lights waiting for the WALK signal. The next, my eyes caught on a man in that crowd, a stranger looking my way, and as the door to the shop opened and the bells above it jingled, I startled like someone had just shouted in my ear.

As my heart began to race and my palms began to sweat, the world around me began to spin out of control.

"You good to go?"

Sean's voice was like a gunshot to my crazed mind, and as I jerked away from him and plastered my back to the dressing room door, Sean stepped in front of me and reached for my arm.

"Xander? Xander? Are you okay?" Sean looked over his shoulder to the window I was transfixed on, and then back to me. "Did you see someone? Someone you've seen before?"

No, I'd never seen him before. He was just some stranger in the crowd who happened to look my way. But then again, that was exactly who would send an anonymous letter, right?

"Do you have a back entrance?" Sean barked at the clerk. "Would you mind if we—"

"No," I finally said, shaking my head. "It's okay. There's nothing out there. It's just my..."

I licked at my dry lips, and Sean narrowed his eyes, his fingers tightening around my arm. The panic from only seconds ago seemed to fade, and I found my words getting stuck around the lump that had formed in the back of my throat.

"It's not okay. *You're* not okay. We're going out the back."

Sean didn't wait for a response. He guided me through the racks of clothes and followed the woman ahead of us until we were pushing through the back exit, and when it slammed shut behind us, I found myself standing in an empty alley.

Sean dumped his bags on the ground by my feet as he looked left and then right. When he seemed happy that we were alone, he came back to where I was standing flush to the brick wall.

What the hell is the matter with me?

"Xander?" Sean's voice was much calmer now, his tone less harsh.

I blinked and tried to swallow around the lump. But when it was clear I still wasn't quite myself, Sean reached out to take either side of my face.

"Hey."

His rough palms against my cheeks made me look at him. When Sean offered up a half-smile that made the corners of his deep blue eyes crease, I felt my panic drain out of me.

"You're okay."

I read Sean's lips, but couldn't quite make out the words as the ringing in my ears continued.

"You had a panic attack."

As I continued to stare at him, mute for probably the first time in my life, Sean stroked one of his thumbs over the curve of my cheek.

"Did you see something, someone watching you?"

"I... No, they weren't watching me, they just..." Sean stroked my cheek again, and this time the spike in my blood pressure had nothing to do with anxiety. I took his hands and gently pulled them from my face. "I'm okay. I just got caught up in my head for a minute there and thought I saw something. It was nothing, I'm sure, just lots of people."

Sean was standing much closer to me than he would under normal circumstances, and when his eyes roamed over my face, I angled my chin up, hoping a show of bravado would make him back off, but I was out of luck.

"That's understandable."

Was it? I'd never had a panic attack before, and I'd been in some pretty hairy situations in the past. Interviews with murderers, dictators—hell, I'd reported from the middle of war zones, for God's sake. Now here I was having a meltdown because some creep sent me a few messages?

Jesus, Xander, get a hold of yourself.

"I'm fine," I said, and straightened from the wall. "But do you mind if we go home now? I think I want to lie down for a bit before we go to Bailey's."

Sean didn't look at all convinced that I wasn't about to fall on my face, so I bent down, picked up his bags, and held them up between us.

"Plus, you're going to need time to decide which of these outfits you're going to wear tonight."

"Uh, I was thinking I'd leave these for Monday."

I shook my head. "Nope. What better audience to try these out on than your brothers? You know they'll be honest."

Sean raised an eyebrow. "Honest? More like they'll give me shit for trying to look like some kind of preppy Holly-wood cop. But okay, I'll do it. Only because you just had a freak-out."

My mouth fell open, but he was right. I'd had a freak-out, and no one was more shocked than me that Sean had been the one to calm me down. The one to...comfort me.

As we walked side by side toward the parking garage on the corner of the street, Sean said, "You got a pair of hair clippers at home?"

"Hair clippers?"

Sean ran a hand through his hair. "I was gonna get it cut, but then I ended up—"

"Coming to work for me?"

He chuckled, and the sound was a welcome relief from the chaos of minutes ago.

"Yeah, I guess I did, huh?"

"Mhmm. And yes, I'm pretty sure I have some somewhere. But if you want to go and get it done—"

Sean stopped and grabbed my arm, halting me. "I'm not leaving you."

You wouldn't think four words would have such an impact, but I could've hugged him for saying them—not that I would ever tell him that.

"Come on, Sean. I think I'll be okay in my house."

Sean took in a deep breath, and then let it out as though he were praying for patience. "Even if I thought that was true, there's no way I'm leaving you after what just happened here."

"That's never happened before."

"And yet today it did. So forget it." Sean started to walk again, and I jogged to catch up. "You best get used to me, Xander, because until this motherfucker is caught, I'm not going anywhere. You got that?"

Yes, I did, and as I fell into silence, I found I'd never been more grateful than I was right then, walking down the street beside pain in the ass Sean Bailey.

WHEN I WOKE LATER that afternoon, the sun was slipping through the blinds I'd lowered when we'd gotten home, and I'd kicked the sheets off me in my fitful sleep.

I couldn't remember any of my dreams, but I could tell by the throbbing headache that they hadn't been peaceful. I glanced at the clock on my bedside and saw it was just turning four—*shit.*

Sean and I had decided to leave around five to get to Bailey's in time for dinner. I slowly sat up and got to my feet, then figured I should probably go and tell him I was awake.

I padded across the hardwood and pulled open my double doors, fully expecting to find Sean waiting where he had been the last two times I'd left this room. But when the hall was empty, something cold skated down my spine.

"Sean?" I called out, and when I got no reply except for the familiar sounds my place always made, my pulse begin to race. "Sean? You out here?"

Again. Nothing.

This was ridiculous. He was probably in the living room and couldn't hear me. But even as I told myself that, I tried to imagine a scenario in which Sean would put enough distance between us that he wouldn't be able to hear my movements. It just didn't seem plausible. Not when he'd been so particular about it from the get-go.

Telling myself there had to be a good explanation as to why he wasn't guarding my bedroom door, I did my best to squash down the lump in my throat and made myself step out of my room.

The first thing I noticed was that his bedroom door was shut, when he usually slept with it open—the guard-dog thing much more effective if you didn't have closed doors between you.

Just as I was about to reach for the handle, I heard a noise from down the hall and yanked my hand back. My heart pounded as I stared down the endlessly long hall, and when I realized it was just the icemaker, I let out a breath.

Fuck. I was a nervous wreck in my own house, jumping at every little damn noise, and I hated it. This was Sean's fault. His *don't think your castle can't be breached* speech had me walking around on fucking eggshells.

Irritated, I raised my hand and knocked on Sean's door, and when I got no answer, I opened it a crack. God knew I didn't want to walk in on him doing anything I'd rather not see. I had enough nightmares to have to deal with that too.

But when I entered the bedroom and found it empty, I frowned.

Where the hell is he? I was about to go in search of him when I heard a faucet in the bathroom turn on and off, and then the door handle jiggled.

Of course, I thought as I watched the door open, *he's getting ready to leave.* And before I could tuck tail and run, Sean stepped out of the bathroom and my jaw nearly hit the floor.

Somewhere between us getting home, me taking a nap, and right now, Sean had made a complete transformation.

Gone was the long hair he'd arrived with two days ago, and in its place were short, tapered sides and thick, textured strands he'd side-swept with his natural cowlick. He'd trimmed his stubble to a fashionable length and dressed in the third outfit he'd tried on today.

Brown boots, designer jeans that fit his long, muscular legs, a simple grey t-shirt, and a distressed leather biker jacket. It made a hell of an impact for a man who usually wore a crumpled suit for work, or five-year old jeans, faded sports shirts, and baseball caps on the regular.

Sean looked like a completely different man, one I'd never seen before, and when he finally spotted me standing there, he tugged at the sleeves of his jacket and frowned.

"So? Do I pass muster? What do you think?"

What did I think? I thought he looked sexy as hell. But I would rather shave my head than admit that, so I decided to ignore his question and go on the defensive instead.

"Did you not hear me a minute ago?"

Sean walked over to me, still fiddling with his cuffs. "Huh? When?"

"You didn't hear me calling your name?"

Sean stopped in front of me and tried shrugging the coat into place. I let out a sigh and reached for the lapels.

"Here," I said, and tugged them neatly into place over his shirt, then smoothed my hands along the supple leather.

He looked down at where my palms were now resting on his chest, and I quickly pulled them back.

"Sorry, didn't hear you. I was using the clippers and then took a quick shower. I thought you'd be sleeping a little longer."

"I said we'd leave at five."

"Right." Sean looked at his watch. "It's only ten after four. You got plenty of time."

"I still need to shower and change."

Sean smiled, and I wasn't sure if it was because of the newly trimmed stubble or the overall makeover, but I found myself zeroing in on his mouth and finding it difficult to look away.

"And that takes you forty-five minutes?"

"At least thirty."

Sean chuckled, and when my traitorous cock responded in a way it *never* did to Sean Bailey, I took a quick step back. "So...I'm going to go."

Sean shrugged. "Okay."

I turned and all but ran to his door, and just as I was about to slip through it and lock myself in my bedroom, I heard him say, "You never said. Do I pass inspection?"

I glanced over my shoulder, and when my dick throbbed again, I gripped the handle a little harder and nodded.

What the hell was going on with me? Was this some kind of residual emotion from this morning? Was I feeling extra affection because Sean had helped me when I needed him?

"You can leave it open," Sean said, as I was about to yank the door shut as though it were some kind of force field between us. "I'm going to be out there in a second."

I didn't want to think about Sean standing outside my door while I got naked and showered. Not when my body was acting like it was on crack. *Jesus.*

So I bolted into my bedroom, locked the door, and headed for a cold shower. Maybe the shock would remind my dick that Sean was the last person it should get excited about.

One thing was certain, though: while I was busy panicking about this, I'd completely forgotten how scared I'd been minutes before. It seemed Sean—whether he was trying to or not—had the innate ability to make me feel safe, among a whole lot of other bizarre feelings.

None of which I planned to examine anytime, well, ever.

16

SEAN

AS WE PULLED into my brothers drive and I cut the engine, I looked over to Xander sitting still and silent, much as he had the entire drive out here. Something was going on with him. What, I had no idea. But ever since he'd woken up this afternoon, he'd been...off.

At first I'd thought it might have to do with what had happened this morning. It was clear he'd been rattled, and while he'd tried to pull it together on our way back to his place, I thought that maybe his sleep hadn't been quite as restful as he'd hoped, and the anxious feelings from earlier had lingered.

But as I took the keys from the ignition and was about to ask him if he was okay, Xander unbuckled his belt and shoved the SUV door open, practically flinging himself out of the vehicle before I had a chance to say shit.

Frowning, I followed suit. Tonight was going to be interesting. I hadn't seen my brothers in weeks, and considering my new makeover, I knew they were going to have a million and one questions that were going to be greatly entertaining for them, and fucking painful for me.

Huh, maybe that's what was wrong with Xander.

"Hey," I called out as Xander booked it up the front drive and I jogged to catch up. "There a fire I don't know about or something? What's the hurry?"

Xander barely spared me a glance as he continued on, and something about the brush-off ruffled my feathers. I thought we'd called a truce today during the shopping and freak-out. But clearly I knew jack shit about Xander and his mood swings, 'cause he was having a hell of a one right now.

"Am I really such bad company you're running to find replacements?"

Xander stopped and turned, and with the slight slope of Bailey's drive he was at eye level with me, something that was rare, considering I had him by a good few inches.

"Don't tell me you aren't feeling the same? We've spent more time together in the last two days than we have in our entire lives."

Something about the way he said that grated on my nerves, and when I crossed my arms and glared him down, Xander held my gaze.

Brave, considering most cowered from that look.

"And that's so fucking terrible for you? Spending time with me," I said.

"Well, it certainly hasn't been a picnic, if that's what you're asking."

Wow, okay. "Yeah, 'cause you're such a walk in the park," I said, and brushed by him, our shoulders bumping a little harder than I'd intended. But fuck it. He was pissing me off.

"What's that supposed to mean?"

I reached Bailey's door, knocked once, then turned and let Xander have it.

"It means that you're a spoiled, ungrateful snob, Xander. You have more mood swings than my mother used to. I don't know what happened between you taking a nap and right now, but the idea of being around other people is the best fucking one I can think of. That way, I'll be less likely to kill you."

Xander's face reddened as though his blood was boiling, and it probably was. But before his head had a chance to explode right off his shoulders, I heard the door open and pivoted to see Bailey, who took one look at me and frowned.

"Sean?"

"Yeah," I said, my voice gruff, my mood now shot to shit.

Bailey chuckled as he took in my new polished getup. "Are you *sure* that's you? It's been a while, and the last time I saw you, you didn't own an iron."

"Hilarious, Bay. Are you gonna open the fucking door? Or just stand there all night gawking at me?"

Bailey continued to laugh as he stepped aside, and when I walked past him and he finally caught sight of Xander behind me, he grinned.

"Oh, hey, Xander. I didn't see you there."

Once inside my childhood home, I looked back to where

Xander remained on the front porch, looking like he wanted to cut and run. But too bad for him, because he didn't have a fucking car.

Bailey peered out the front door at his drive, and when all he saw was my SUV, he looked between the two of us. "Did you Uber here? I could've come and gotten you if something's wrong with your car."

When Xander didn't answer, I wondered what exactly was going through his head—probably thoughts on the best way to kill me.

We'd already discussed telling Bailey what was going on tonight, so I figured we might as well start now. If Xander didn't like it, well, he could add it to the list of my shortcomings he was clearly keeping in his mind.

"Xander came with me."

Xander coughed, the first sound he'd made since his verbal sparring match with me.

"Came with you?" Bailey said. "What do you mean he came with you?"

Xander muttered something unintelligible as he marched forward and shoved me out of the way.

"We have to talk," he said to Bailey as though I wasn't even there. "But first I need to eat, because I plan to drink—a lot."

"Okay..." Bailey said as we all moved out of the doorway and he closed the door behind us. "Henri's in the kitchen. Kieran got caught at work tonight, so it's just the four of us. You can go through. Sean, would you like me to hang your coat for you?"

I glared at my brother, shrugged out of my coat, and tossed it over the back of his couch. "I'm just fine, thanks. But I need a fucking bourbon, stat."

If ever a night called for me to have a drink, then this was it.

17

XANDER

ABOUT AN HOUR into dinner at Bailey's, I was feeling good and buzzed courtesy of the drinks Henri kept bringing my way whenever I was about to hit empty.

I'd made it my mission to keep as far away from Sean as possible since the verbal dress-down he'd given me outside, and if *why* I'd been so quiet on the way over here wasn't so damn mortifying, I might've told the jackass to pull his fucking head in.

As it was, I wasn't about to admit I was avoiding him because I couldn't seem to control my cock whenever he was near. That just seemed like a fate worse than death—not that that was the best analogy for me these days either.

"Running a little low there, Xander. Need another?"

I turned to see Henri crossing the large deck in his usual boots, faded jeans, and black tee. He had a bottle of the good stuff in his hand, and as much as I wanted to say yes to another refill, I knew I needed to slow it down.

"I'm fine for now, thanks."

Henri shrugged and placed the bottle on the rail behind him. "No problem. You've been hitting it kinda hard since you got here anyway. Something up?"

Bad choice of words right there, and as my eyes cut to the grill where Sean stood with Bailey, I shook my head.

Henri chuckled. "Wanna maybe try that again with more conviction?"

The twinkle in his eyes almost matched the twinkle from the small silver piercing through his nose, and told me I wasn't fooling anyone, especially him.

Henri Boudreaux had come into all our lives around six months ago. He'd started out as a CI for Sean after being arrested—who, we'd all been told, was a complete delight to work with. Not.

But then fate had stepped in, a traffic ticket was issued by Bailey, and bam, the man who had once lived a life of ill repute was now on the straight and narrow with my best friend—well, the narrow, at least.

Turned out him and Bailey were perfect for one another, and I couldn't be happier for them.

"I've just been dealing with some crazy stuff this week and it's taking its toll, that's all," I said.

Henri frowned. "What kind of stuff?"

"Work stuff."

Sean looked up at that moment and pinned me with a look that made my fingers tighten around my tumbler. Shit, how was it that I was so aware of him now? How tall he was,

How broad-shouldered. How good those jeans looked cupping his—

I quickly dragged my eyes back up to see Sean now scowling at Henri. Clearly that relationship was still in progress.

As Sean went back to talking with Bailey, Henri leaned into me, bumping shoulders. "Wanna tell me what that was about?"

"What what was about?"

"Nice try. But I happen to know you're way smarter than that. So what's going on with you and Dick? And what's with this...new version of him? He almost looks human."

Just hearing Henri put us together in the same sentence, as though we belonged there, was all kinds of wrong. I raised my glass to drain the remainder of my bourbon, and just as I was about to swallow, Henri said, "You two fucking?"

I nearly choked on the alcohol but somehow managed to force it down and get control of my coughing fit. "What?"

"Are you two—"

"I heard you."

"Well?"

"No. He's straight." When Henri's eyes widened, I realized how that sounded. As in, if Sean wasn't straight, we would be? Hell no. "Plus it's *Sean*. No. I just... We—" *Fuck. Spit it out already, Xander.* "He's helping me out with something. We need to talk to you guys about it later, but it's complicated and weird."

"More complicated than if you were—"

"*Don't* say it again," I said, pointing at Henri's chest.

Henri laughed and held up his hands. "Okay, I'm just sayin'. That'd be really fucking weird. Especially for Bailey, right?"

"I think you need to stop talking about this or I'm going to lose all my alcohol on your boots."

"Shit, don't do that. They're new."

"Okay, guys," Bailey called out as he handed Sean the tray of steaks and closed the lid of the grill. "Get your asses to the table."

As we headed toward the sliding back door, Sean looked over at the two of us, a frown twisting his lips.

I knew he was pissed—or *still* pissed—about what I'd said on needing company other than him, but it was for the best. Being around Sean, and only Sean, these last few days had caused some anomaly in my brain and body, and there was no way I was going to add fuel to the fire by being close to him around his family.

Like Henri said, it'd be really weird if something I couldn't control should happen, leaving me to explain my wayward cock to my best friend and his brother.

It was just best, for now, if Sean hated me. That way, things would go back to normal...right?

18

SEAN

XANDER WASN'T LYING about wanting to spend time with people other than me, and about two hours into the evening I was just about fucking done with it.

I knew the two of us weren't the best of friends—whatever the hell that meant—but did he really find me so repellent he needed a time-out?

I wasn't one to usually give a shit under normal circumstances, but it annoyed me to no end that I was fixated on his little avoidance routine tonight, and after we'd all finished eating and I saw him stacking up Bailey's plates to take them into the kitchen, I got to my feet and picked up several glasses to follow.

With Bailey and Boudreaux safely tucked away in the living room all kissy face, I made my way to where Xander was rinsing the dishes for the dishwasher.

Earlier I'd caught him talking with Boudreaux out on

the deck, and something about the way they'd been watching me told me I'd been the topic under discussion.

At first, I'd thought Xander had been filling him in on what had happened this week. But I dismissed that idea when Boudreaux started laughing and Xander looked like he wanted to disappear into thin air.

So...maybe he'd mentioned the cover story? That would no doubt tickle Boudreaux's funny bone—the idea of me playing a gay man. But again, if that was the reason why Xander looked so fucking offended, I was just about done.

I was doing him a favor, for fuck's sake. He didn't have to act like I had the goddamn plague.

Just as that thought entered my head, I put the glasses down on the kitchen counter and said, "Okay, what the hell is going on with you tonight?"

I didn't have to be a detective to notice the way Xander's spine stiffened, and when he straightened his shoulders and glanced back at me, my stomach did some weird flipping thing.

Oh shit, Bailey better have cooked that steak all the way through.

"Nothing is going on with me tonight."

"Bullfuckingshit." I leaned against the counter by the sink. "You've hardly said two words to me all night."

"That's not true." Xander went back to rinsing plates. "I just said seven."

I reached across him and flicked off the water, and when he glared at me, I realized how close that put us to one another. Our sides were touching and our faces were within inches of each other.

"What'd I do to piss you off so bad?"

Xander's chest rose and fell against my arm. "Can you please move out of the way?" he said, polite as ever.

Pulling my arm back, I slid a little way down the counter and crossed my arms. "Come on, Xander. What's going on? Is it because of this morning? I know it was rough, but I'm not going to tell anyone, if that's what you're worried about."

Xander shut his eyes and took in a deep breath, and as he let it out he flicked off the water and turned to look at me. "It's not that."

"It's not?"

"No."

"Okay." I ran a hand through my hair and gripped the back of my neck. "Then what is it? Because as far as *this* all goes," I said, waving a hand between us, "I thought I was doing pretty damn good. You said the clothes were better."

"They are."

"Then what's the problem? I don't remember saying anything particularly offensive today. We went shopping, what happened happened, you took a nap, and when you woke up, I was getting ready to go out with you. What the fuck happened between now and then?" And why did I suddenly care?

Xander swallowed, and just when he was about to answer, Bailey walked into the kitchen carrying the rest of the glasses.

"You two need some help?"

"I... Uh, I think we have it," Xander said, going back to rinsing the plates.

Bailey pulled open the door to the dishwasher. "You could at least stack the dishes, Sean."

Yeah, shit, I guess I could. But I'd been so focused on trying to work out why Xander was pissed at me that it hadn't even occurred to me.

"So what's been going on with you?" Bailey said as he handed Xander a glass. "You were super quiet at dinner."

I was this close to saying "see" like we were still a bunch of teenagers, when Xander shrugged and said, "Who could get a word in edgewise with Sean talking the whole time?"

"Hey, you could've shut me up anytime you wanted to." Xander pinned me with a look so fierce that I was surprised it didn't cut me off at the knees. "And anyway, seemed no one else had shit to say, so I figured I'd keep you all entertained."

Bailey chuckled. "Yeah, I'm not sure how we survived all these weeks without you. I will say, though, you're looking good, Sean. Or maybe that's because I haven't seen you in a couple of weeks."

I glanced down at my new and improved wardrobe, and figured now was as good a time as any to fill Bailey in on what was really going on.

"Nah, I think that's probably 'cause of Xander."

Xander's hands froze in the sink.

"Because of Xander?" Bailey looked between us, but it wasn't lost on me that Xander had glued his eyes to the glass in his hands.

"Yeah. We need to talk to you, Bay." I tapped Xander's shoulder to make sure he was on board with this, and when he looked over at me and nodded, I turned back to my brother. "Why don't you let us finish up in here, and then we'll come and talk to you and Boudreaux."

Bailey narrowed his eyes. "Is everything...okay?"

I shoved off the counter and clapped him on the shoulder. "Everything's okay. Xander just needed some help, that's all."

"Help?"

Xander turned off the faucet and grabbed the dishtowel to wipe his hands as he turned to face Bailey.

"What kind of help?"

"Let's go and talk." Xander threw the towel on the counter, and we all walked out of the kitchen to find the table cleared and Boudreaux sitting in the living room. He looked at the three of us and said, "Okay, what'd I miss in the kitchen?"

"Nothing," I said, as I walked to the wide windows that overlooked the back of the property, and Bailey sat by Boudreaux's side.

Xander took the recliner, looking about as comfortable as one might sitting in a dentist's chair. So I decided to save him the difficulty of explaining this all over again.

"Earlier this week, Xander received some pretty disturbing threats at his work," I said.

Bailey's eyes flicked from me to his friend, concern crossing his face—along with a whole lot of confusion. "Threats? As in messages?"

"Yes." Xander nodded. "Three of them."

"Each one more personal and more...threatening than the last," I added.

"Oh my God." Bailey scooted forward to the edge of the couch. "Are you okay? Do you know who's sending them?"

"Yes, I'm okay, and no, not yet." Xander wiped his palms on his thighs, and I walked over and stood behind the recliner, hoping to ease some of his nerves.

"If you needed help," Boudreaux said, "Bailey and I could've—"

"No." Xander shook his head. "I mean, I appreciate it, and I did think about it. But my boss wanted me to hire a bodyguard, and you guys just moved in together and I wasn't about to ask one of you to come move in with me, so—"

"Sean moved in with you instead?"

I aimed my best *shut the fuck up* stare at Boudreaux. But clearly the days where I had any clout over him were long gone, because he smirked.

Xander nodded. "It was the smartest move after we talked it through."

"Wait a minute." Bailey got to his feet and looked at me. "You're working as Xander's bodyguard? What about your job?"

"I was already due for a vacation, so I decided to make it a working one," I said.

"Oh, okay. Well, that's good." Bailey turned to Xander. "Sean is an incredible detective. You couldn't be safer."

Those words coming from Bailey made my chest

tighten. I couldn't remember him ever saying something so positive about me before. I looked at Xander, who nodded.

"I know," he said. "That's why I said yes. But that's not all."

Boudreaux chuckled, as if he'd known all along there was more to this than me hiring on as Xander's bodyguard—and fuck him for being right.

"What do you mean?" Bailey said, and then looked over his shoulder at Boudreaux. "Did you know about this?"

Boudreaux—the arrogant fucker—shook his head and grinned at me. "No. But I think it explains Dick's new wardrobe."

"Fuck you, Boudreaux."

"Mmm, I think I'll pass."

"Would you two quit it," Bailey interrupted, and then looked back to Xander. "I want to know what's going on."

When it became clear Xander wasn't about to tell him, I let out a breath said, "Because we don't want to scare this psycho off before we catch him, we had to come up with a reason for why I would be around Xander twenty-four seven."

"Right, like undercover? You do that all the time."

"Exactly."

"So what'd you come up with?" Bailey asked, still not cluing in. Not that I blamed him—this really was the last scenario he would ever think of.

"Bet I know."

At Boudreaux's comment, I dug my fingers into the back of the recliner. "Did anyone ask you?"

"No. But Bailey's asking you. So why don't you tell him?" The direct challenge in Boudreaux's voice was all for me, that I was sure of. But knowing this was going to be uncomfortable for Xander made my anger rise.

"Why don't you back the fuck off? We're getting there, okay?"

Bailey's head jerked in my direction, but I was zeroed in on Boudreaux, who inclined his head ever so slightly.

Was that an apology? I wasn't sure, but if it was, I knew it was more for Xander than myself.

"Bay," Xander finally said, "this is going to be as weird for you as it is for me, I'm sure. But after running through all the scenarios, the best way for Sean to be around me all the time without question was to have him go undercover as my boyfriend."

You could've heard a pin drop with how quiet the room got, and then Bailey blinked and looked between us.

"You're going to pretend to date...Xander?"

I was about to tell him yes, and not to be upset because it should be over pretty soon, when Bailey let out the loudest laugh I'd heard from him in years.

"You're going to..." Still laughing, Bailey looked to Boudreaux, who was grinning. "Sean's going to..." Bailey shook his head and whirled back around to face me. "You're going to pretend to be *gay*?"

Bailey completely lost it, laughing so hard that tears came out his eyes, and once he finally got himself under some kind of control, he said, "I'm sorry. I just— Really? That's—"

"Insane? Right?" Xander shot to his feet. "As if anyone's going to believe *Sean* is gay. I told him that."

Bailey let out another laugh and came around the coffee table to rub Xander's arm. "I'm so sorry. This has had to have been so horrible for you."

"Hey, I'm right here, you know," I said. "And I think I've been doing a pretty good job, all things considered."

Xander glanced over his shoulder at me and grimaced. "I tried to make him more...dateable?"

Bailey snorted. "It definitely shows, but come on, it's Sean. He's not really your type."

Okay, apparently I was fucking invisible, the two of them now talking as though I wasn't even there. Xander finally had someone to commiserate with over what a bad idea this had all been.

I gritted my teeth, trying to bite back any scathing comments, when Boudreaux got to his feet and came around the recliner to me.

"I'd ask if you need any tips on how to act around Xander to make this little charade of yours more believable." Boudreaux looked over to where Bailey and Xander were still busy discussing what a horrible option I was, and then added, "But I think you know how act with him better than he even realizes."

I whipped my head to the side to see Boudreaux's lips twitching. But before I could tell him to fuck off, he clapped me on the back *hard* and said, "Be careful there, Dick. I think this job is much more dangerous than you think."

The fuck? I'd been up against some of the most ruthless

drug cartels in the country, not to mention gangs and murderers. Boudreaux was delusional if he thought this was more dangerous.

But before I could tell him he was totally off the mark, Boudreaux headed to the kitchen, leaving me under the scrutiny of two men who had decided the rest of the night would be finishing the makeover Xander had begun earlier in the day.

19

XANDER

"AND WE'RE BACK in five, four, three..." Two and one were mouthed by Mikey behind camera one as the lead-in music rolled and the red light on the camera turned green.

"Our final story tonight is one that should put a smile on your face. NASA astronaut Linda Hastings made history today as she came back to earth after spending a total of three hundred and twenty-eight days in space—the most time ever for a female. She was greeted by hundreds of people upon arrival, but there was only one hug, one reaction, she wanted more than any other."

The broadcast switched to the footage of Linda returning home to her dog, wagging its tail so hard its butt almost flew right off, and after about a million puppy dog kisses and hugs, it was clear her little dog, who had been waiting a year—seven in his mind—hadn't forgotten its owner.

The footage finished, and when the camera switched

back to me, I couldn't help the smile on my face as I wrapped up the broadcast.

"We could watch that all night. But for now, that's all from us here at Global News on this lovely Tuesday evening. I'm Alexander Thorne. Thank you for watching, and good night."

The red light flicked on above the camera, and as Mikey gave me the signal we were clear, I pulled my earpiece free. Jim had been chattering to the graphics producer about tweaking something for tomorrow night's show, but if he didn't need me, I was out.

This week was taking forever. It felt like it should be Friday already, and we were only halfway in. It made sense that time would drag though when you were constantly monitoring your every move. But when nothing even remotely alarming or out of place had occurred, I was starting to think that this was all a colossal waste of time.

I pushed out of the studio, unclipped my mic, and handed it off to Ryan as we walked through the desks on the way to my office.

"If anyone needs me, I'll be here for another thirty minutes. Maybe."

"No problem, boss."

"And if anyone calls for me and it's not an emergency—"

"Take a message and tell you tomorrow."

I nodded and loosened my tie as I walked through my office door, ready to get out of my suit for the day. I tossed the tie toward my desk and someone caught it, and my heart close to flew out of my chest. "*Shit.*"

Sean was lounging back in my office chair with his feet propped up on a filing cabinet, one ankle over the other. I hadn't seen or heard from him since he'd dropped me at ENN's front door, valet style, this morning at around eleven.

"Hey, babe."

Babe? Okay, that was new, and needed to never be said again by Sean. But in the spirit of keeping up this ridiculous act in front of Ryan, I offered up my biggest smile and responded the best I could.

"Hey yourself. I didn't know you were going to meet me after work tonight."

Sean looked over my shoulder to Ryan. "I wanted it to be a surprise."

A surprise? He'd scared the living daylights out of me. "That's nice."

Sean's lips twitched. He'd clearly gotten the message that I thought it was anything but. "You know me, always trying to be nice."

I couldn't help but scoff, because of all the words I'd use to describe Sean Bailey, *nice* was not one of them.

"I'll be back in a few for your suit," Ryan cut in, and that was when I realized he thought I'd have no problem stripping in front of my "boyfriend" so my suit could be laundered.

But after Sean's eyes wandered down over me, and that unwanted sensation I'd managed to bank since last Saturday resurfaced, I turned to Ryan and said, "That's okay. I didn't realize Sean was meeting me, so we'll just head out now for dinner. I'll send this one off myself."

"You sure?"

"Positive. You can head home. I'll see you tomorrow."

Ryan looked around my shoulder, a wide grin on his face. "Hey, you can come around more often if it means I get to leave early."

It took all I had not to roll my eyes, as if Sean needed any more encouragement to be here. "Thanks. I just might do that. Have a good one, Ryan."

"You too." Ryan waved and then disappeared out the door, and as it slowly shut behind him, I turned on Sean.

"*Babe?*"

Sean shrugged and sat up. "Eh, I was trying it out. It didn't really feel right for me either."

I couldn't help but laugh, because seriously, the endearment was too soft, too sweet, for someone like Sean.

"Glad that's settled."

"How 'bout sweet cheeks? Honey? Silver fox?"

"Silver— How about no, no, and definitely not." I walked over to take my tie from him, and as I reached out, Sean tightened his grip.

"Everything go smoothly today?" Sean's voice had gone from light and teasing to serious in seconds, and the direct way he was looking into my eyes made my heart beat a little faster. "There was nothing unusual around the office or in the studio, from what I could see. Anything happen with you I should know about?"

I shook my head. "No. I'm starting to feel like I'm wasting your time."

Sean's eyes narrowed, and when he tugged on the tie, I had to brace my hand on the desk to not fall flat on my face.

"Listen to me: you are not wasting my time. First, your company is paying me the equivalent of a year's salary to be here. That's a lot of fucking money. Second, this is exactly what I figured would happen. You see, your little stalker friend has probably noticed you're walking around with a hot new piece of ass these days, and is trying to work out his next move. Don't become complacent, and *never* think you're wasting my time."

The intensity of Sean's words made mine get stuck in my throat, and when he let go of the tie and got to his feet, I too straightened.

Sean came out from behind the desk, and I took in the new and improved version of him as he stopped in front of me. Over the last three days, those crumpled suits, tattered jeans, and ripped sports shirts had become a thing of the past, and in their place were fitted black slacks, a navy button-up shirt, and black sports jacket that fit him to perfection.

He seemed like a whole new person—until, of course, he opened his mouth.

"So what's this about you taking me to dinner?"

"Excuse me?"

"You told Ryan you were taking me to dinner."

"No. I told him a lie to get him out of here."

"Oh, well, I'm pretty fucking hungry. Did you eat?"

I hadn't, actually, now that he mentioned it. "Not yet. But don't think I'm buying you dinner. You use my hot water each night and sleep under my roof. You can buy *me* dinner."

Sean sized me up and then nodded. "Fair enough. But we don't have to eat sushi or some bullshit meal, right?"

"Let me guess, you want a nice, thick slab of meat to sink your teeth into. Would you like to hunt it down and shoot it too?"

"Do they offer that option in town?"

I rolled my eyes and walked around the desk to grab my keys and wallet from my top drawer.

"Seriously, though," Sean said. "Do you feel like a steak?"

I could go for a steak, but... "As long as it's not at a sports bar." When Sean opened his mouth as if to offer up an alternative, I added, "And not some local pub that you and all your police pals go to."

"If there's one of those, I don't know about it."

"Oh, come on. Bailey had tons of friends on the force. So did your father. Are you trying to tell me you have none? What do you do for fun?"

"Fun?"

"Yes. You know, the activity you do that makes you happy and smile." As Sean stared blankly at me, I shook my head and checked my email on my phone. "Right, I forgot who I was talking to."

"Hey, I know how to have fun. I just don't really have time these days. My life isn't all rosy and shit, you know. I spend most of my days talking to dead people."

"Wait...you see ghosts? Are there any in here now?"

"Yeah, yeah, laugh it up. But I figure if anyone knows how depressing life can be, it would be you. You see the bad shit almost as much as I do. You even get to tell the country about it."

"Hence the fun."

"Yeah, I can see you're *so* good at having that."

I sighed and slipped my phone into my pocket. "Okay, let's go and get something to eat. I need to get out of these confined quarters, otherwise I can't be held responsible for what I might do to you in the next five minutes or so."

Sean pulled open the door with a flourish and gestured for me to go ahead, and as I brushed by him and noticed his cologne, that...unexpected sensation below my belt hit again and made me walk a little bit faster out my office door.

20

SEAN

IT WAS BUSY downtown for a Tuesday night. Much busier now than it had been when we'd arrived at McNally's Steakhouse. Not that that was surprising, considering the extra hours of light and the warm summer nights. But as we stepped out of the restaurant, I wished it was a blizzard and everyone was home. That way it'd be easier to keep an eye on anything unusual happening around us.

As it was, though, Xander was right. It had been quiet since I'd arrived on the scene to watch over him. But I'd expected that, especially if this nutjob was as obsessed with Xander as those messages indicated.

He—or she—was no doubt pissed off right now to see the object of their infatuation out and about with a new somebody. And being on the crowded streets of Chicago with that notion at the forefront in my mind made me extra fucking twitchy.

"You ready to go home now, Prince Charming? I think it

might be smart if we get out of here and head somewhere less crowded."

"Why? Did you see something?" Xander quickly scanned the area directly around him, and I didn't miss that his eyes were a little wider.

"No. It's just much busier now than when we arrived. So if there's nowhere else you'd like to go, I think we should head back to the car."

Xander looked over to where we'd snagged a parking spot earlier and nodded. "Yes, okay. You're right. And there's nowhere I need to go. Although I might hit my tread-mill when I get home after the amount I just ate."

I chuckled. Leave it to Xander to worry about his looks while I was worrying about his damn life.

"I hardly think that tiny filet mignon is going to ruin your body. But if you wanna run it off when we get home, I'm happy to sit in the corner and keep watch. There's no way you're getting me on a treadmill after that porterhouse —if anything, I'm gonna hit a food coma."

Xander scoffed. "Good to know my life will be in the hands of a comatose invalid."

Speaking of hands... I held mine out, and Xander took it without question.

"You bet your ass it is," I said, and tugged him into my side. "And I will do everything in my power to keep you alive. No matter how many times you manage to insult me in the space of five minutes."

Xander looked me in the eye, and the faith and trust I saw made my stomach twist. Because no matter how much we argued, no matter how much we bickered, Xander trusted me to keep him safe. He trusted me with his life. I only hoped that I was able to live up to that trust.

"You ready?"

Xander nodded and squeezed my hand. We walked to the edge of the road and stopped to check both ways. Once I was happy there were no oncoming vehicles, we stepped out and started across.

We made it to the middle and made sure things were all clear, but as we stepped off the divider, I heard it.

The revving of an engine.

The squealing of tires.

The snarl of a motor being pushed to its limit, as headlights flashed on and blinded us.

It only took seconds after that. The vehicle barreled down the road at a hellacious pace, its aim clear, its target in sight, and just when it would've hit the two of us, I threw all my weight into Xander, shoving him off the road.

As we fell toward the pavement, I wrapped my arms around him to keep him covered. We hit the ground with a loud *thwack*, and as the screeching sound of tires filled the night air, I arched up, trying to get a glimpse of the license plate as it disappeared into the night.

G35—something, something, fuck. *I didn't catch the rest.*

Xander had my hand in a death grip and clutched my jacket's lapel, and when I realized there was shit all I could do to go after the motherfucker, I paid attention to what I *could* do—take care of Xander.

"You all right?" I asked. Xander nodded, but as I went to move away, he gripped me tighter. "Xander?"

"Give me a minute," he said, his breathing harsh and ragged as he lay sprawled beneath me, and the terror in his eyes matched the fear in my heart. Because never in all my life had I been as scared as when I saw that car coming for him. "I just need a minute."

I placed a hand on the pavement by his head to try to keep some of my weight off him, and that was when I saw several people crossing the road to come to our aid. "I'm not sure you're gonna have a minute, Mr. Anchorman. People are headed this way."

Xander blinked up at me, his eyes dazed. "You...you saved me."

He sounded so bewildered that I couldn't help but smile. "Well, that is why you hired me, right? Not for my charming personality."

Xander took in a shaky breath, and as his body came into full contact with mine, I felt something hard brush up against my thigh, something I'd never felt before.

I looked down between us, and Xander cursed, trying to shift out of my grasp. But I held him still and shook my head.

"It's okay."

Xander said nothing, but his cheeks were now a flaming red.

"It's the adrenaline. That's all. Nothing to be ashamed about."

Xander bit down on his lower lip and nodded. "Can you, umm, move now? If you think it's safe."

I studied him closely and could see the humiliation stamped all over his face. Not wanting passersby to gawk, I pushed up to my feet and offered a hand.

Xander looked at it, then at me, and, not wanting to cause him any more discomfort this evening, I schooled my expression to serious. He reached up, and as I helped him to his feet, I pushed the key fob for the SUV.

I ushered him inside the car and closed the door behind him, and as I stared through the window at his profile, I couldn't help but notice a stirring south of my belt.

What the...? Adrenaline? Yeah, that's all it was. I quickly shoved it aside and rounded the SUV to the driver's side. I needed to get Xander somewhere safe and secure. The last thing I needed to worry about was something I had no control over.

It was just the moment, the rush. It was a natural reaction. Just like I'd told Xander. But if it was so natural, why had it never happened before?

21

SEAN

"GOOD MORNING..."

XANDER'S familiar voice floated across the air and found me where I stood looking out at Lake Michigan. I knew that voice almost as well as my own. As a delicious warmth infused my body, I closed my eyes and thought back to last night. Back to the moment Xander had invited me to his bed.

Damn, he'd been something else. Unlike anyone I'd ever had before. The way his body had fit against mine, the way he'd moved as though he couldn't get enough of me. Even now, the memory of it made an insatiable hunger claw at my insides, and as I turned to see him walking into the living room, my cock jerked.

Fuck, he was hot. How had I never noticed that before? But in nothing but a pair of silky, low-slung grey pants, I found it difficult to look anywhere but at him.

"You left me," he said as he came closer, his bare feet

just as much a draw for my eyes as his chest, arms, and that famous face of his. "Not having second thoughts, are you?"

"Not one."

Those full lips, the ones that had demolished all doubt and brought pleasure so intense that my mind was still reeling, curved. "So you want to do it again? Is that what you're trying to say?"

I reached for him, because there was no way in hell I could stop myself. I tugged him forward and took his chin in my hand, then lowered my head to whisper across his lips, "I want do it over and *over* again."

Xander groaned and grabbed at my hips. Then he rocked up against me, and his stiff shaft came into contact with mine. The pleasure was unreal, unlike anything I'd ever experienced before. Then he slipped a hand beneath my sweats to curl his fingers around my—

FUCK.

I JACK-KNIFED up in bed as reality crashed in and woke me from my dream, and as I looked around the room, trying to place myself, I realized that I was in my bed, in Xander's house, alone. *Thank God.*

My breathing came in rapid bursts, and I was well aware of the insistent throb between my thighs. And as I thought about the man in the room next door, it increased in intensity.

Holy shit. I pressed the heel of my hand against my

confused cock and shut my eyes, but then Xander's lips and sea-green eyes appeared.

Jesus. What the hell was going on with me? In all the years that I'd known Xander, I'd never thought of him in a sexual manner. *Any* guy, for that matter. But as I shoved the sheet aside and looked down at my lap, there was no mistaking what was going on there.

Okay, Sean, I told myself. *Just breathe and think about something else. Your body is just reacting to everything that happened last night. White-knight syndrome and all that.*

But even if that was true, when was the last time I'd gotten a hard-on from doing my goddamn job? How about never?

I leaned back against the headboard and scrubbed my hands over my face. This was crazy. Maybe Xander had been right all along and it was a bad idea mixing our history and...friendship this way. Maybe I was too close to be objective and play the role I needed to. That much was obvious if I was having sex dreams about him now.

I sighed and looked at the time: four a.m. Xander would be up in about an hour, and I needed to get my head in order if I had any hope of acting like everything was okay. The last thing I needed was to be all weird and shit after the scare he'd had last night. He needed me to be strong, professional, and I could do that.

I would do a quick sweep of the place now, then grab a shower and meet him when he woke, and everything would go back to normal.

I was sure of it.

22

XANDER

THANK GOD FOR caffeine. Glorious, glorious *caffeine.*

I inhaled the freshly brewed coffee and stared out at the city below, thinking how strange it had been to open my bedroom door this morning and find Sean nowhere in sight.

In all fairness, I had been a little early, and he had left a note on my door: *House is clear. I'll be out soon.* So maybe he was sleeping in. If his night was anything like mine, I wouldn't be surprised.

I hadn't slept a wink after what had happened. But as I stared down at the city below, I was cognizant of the fact that it wasn't just the shock of the attempted hit-and-run that had kept me awake, but what had happened *after* that.

Stupid. That was how I felt. We had nearly been mowed down last night, and all I could focus on was how it had felt lying beneath Sean on the concrete.

He had brushed it off, of course. Why wouldn't he? He'd probably dealt with this kind of thing before. Women and men he'd saved, developing some kind of crush or...fixation. Plus, it wasn't like he had any delusions that I was hot for him. This was *Sean*, for heaven's sake.

The problem was that my body seemed to conveniently forget that whenever he was near lately, and instead was focusing on how warm his hand was when it took mine, and how strong and brave he was whenever he talked about being here to protect me.

Hell, maybe I was developing some kind of damsel-in-distress fetish. That was the only reasonable explanation as to why I was suddenly hyperaware—and strangely attracted to—a man I'd spent most of my life barely tolerating. It had to be residual emotions from last night. A thing for my mind to focus on so panic and paranoia wouldn't set in. But that didn't explain last weekend at Bailey's.

Pushing those thoughts aside, I blew the top of my coffee and took my first sip, and as the strong flavor hit my tongue, I hummed in the back of my throat.

Damn, I needed that. With my nerves shot and my mind scrambled, I had a feeling that by the end of the day several cups of this were going to be the only things keeping me going.

"You're up earlier than usual."

I turned to see Sean walking into the kitchen in those loose navy sweats and CPD t-shirt, and if I'd been hoping to feel nothing—or at least idiotic for being aroused by him last night—I was in for disappointment.

The second I took in the sight of the way his chest and arms filled out his shirt, my erection began to throb. *Shit.*

"Xander?"

When I didn't immediately answer, Sean started around the end of the kitchen counter.

"Have trouble sleeping?"

"I, uh...yes. I couldn't sleep."

Sean's brow pinched. "Are you okay?"

Other than suddenly finding you irresistible, and some creep stalking me? Sure, I'm fine.

"Xander?"

"Yes. Sorry. I'm fine. Just everything that happened last night, that's all."

"That's understandable."

I nodded but couldn't seem to find my tongue to respond. God, this was mortifying. Why was my body reacting this way? And why to Sean?

Sean, *for God's sake.*

Silence filled the room, and I took a sip of my coffee for something to do as Sean headed back into the kitchen.

As he got a mug out, then the milk and sugar, I continued to watch him, trying to work out what it was that had shifted in the universe to suddenly make me see Sean as anything other than an annoying presence.

But the more I watched, the more I felt this absurd desire to move closer to him. Like I was tethered to some pulley that was drawing me closer whether I wanted to go or not.

"So I called up a buddy of mine, Nichols, from the station last night when you went to bed," Sean said as he reached for the pot and poured some coffee. "I didn't get the entire plate, but I got a good chunk of it, so we'll see if he can dig anything up."

His back was still to me, and as I walked across my living room, my eyes traveled down the long line of his back to his trim waist, and when they kept going to his surprisingly tight ass, I ran into the side of my couch. "Shit."

As my coffee slopped over the rim of my mug and onto my lustrous white rug, I cursed again and put it down on the end table.

"What happened?"

"Just bring me some paper towels. Hurry."

He tore off a good wad of paper, and when he held it out to me, I looked up just in time to see I was directly in line with the crotch of his sweats.

I jerked back as though he were going to hit me, and when Sean frowned and leaned forward, thrusting the paper in my face, I told myself to snap the hell out of it and took it from him.

"Thanks," I muttered, and started to blot up the coffee. This was going to be hell to get out. I'd need to call someone, have it professionally cleaned.

"What happened? You trip over your own feet?"

I shut my eyes and sighed. "Something like that."

"Hey."

With the paper towel still soaking up the moisture, I raised my head but didn't open my eyes until I knew they were safely above Sean's waistline. "Yes?"

Sean crouched down until we were face to face, and as his eyes roved over me, I bristled under the attention.

Honestly, though, what was I afraid of? That he could read my mind? Hardly. And there was no way on God's green earth that Sean would ever suspect me of having spilt my coffee because I was checking him out.

So I needed to relax. I needed to fucking breathe.

"Last night still got you jumpy?"

Yes. One part more than the other, apparently. But thankfully, I was aware enough to stop those words from tumbling out of my mouth. "I guess so."

Sean nodded and moved the paper over a little to where the liquid was spreading. "If it's any consolation, it shook me up too."

"Really? You seemed pretty together to me." I gathered up the towel and sat back on my heels. "In fact, if it wasn't for you and your quick thinking, I wouldn't have been here to ruin my overly expensive rug now, would I?"

Sean chuckled, and the sound was familiar, warm, and... comforting. "I suppose not. But I want you to know, nothing's going to hurt you, okay?"

"I—"

"Listen." Sean took hold of my wrist. "They have to get through me to get to you, and I'm not about to let that happen."

The sincerity of his words was staggering, as was the realization that if Sean were to put himself between me and danger, then his brothers—two men I considered my family —would be minus someone they loved, and I couldn't fathom that.

"I know you were hoping this lunatic was gone, that he'd

decided to move on, since we hadn't heard anything from him. But I was waiting for this, Xander. Waiting for him to make a move so I would have something solid to investigate and dig a little deeper on."

I let out the breath I hadn't realized I'd been holding. "I understand that. It's just..." I tried to think of the best way to say it.

"What? What is it? And don't say nothing. There's a reason you didn't sleep last night, and I want to know what it is."

"I was just going to say that I don't want to be responsible for you getting hurt. I'd never forgive myself."

Sean's lips curled into the smirk that usually coincided with a remark that made me want to punch him. But instead of dreading what was about to fly out of his mouth, I felt my pulse begin to flutter.

"Aww. Are you admitting that you might like having me around a little?"

Despite the early hour, the coffee stain on my rug, and the fact that my body was doing things that might lead to eventual therapy, I laughed. "I wouldn't go *that* far. You sure that car didn't clip you last night? Maybe in the head?"

Sean straightened to his feet and held his hand out to me for the second time in less than twenty-four hours, and as I took it and stood, he said, "My head's just fine. It's *yours* we need to worry about."

He took the soaked towels from me and headed back to the kitchen, leaving me thinking he just might be right.

Maybe I did get clipped in the head, and that was why my body was acting this way.

But that still didn't explain last weekend, did it?

Yes, I had a feeling that a lot of therapy was in my future.

23

SEAN

MARCUS ST. JAMES was one seriously cool customer. From the second I'd stepped into his office last week, to right now, as he stared me down from behind steepled fingers, I felt like I was about to be reprimanded by my commander down at the precinct.

There was no warmth about the guy, no welcome in his eyes, and as far as I could tell, he was straight-up business, and serious business at that.

"You said you got a license plate?" Marcus's tone was cool and, I was sure, intimidating to most, but if he thought I was about to piss my pants over the likes of him, he had another thing coming.

"I got half a license plate. My guys are working on it."

"And Xander? How is he today?"

I thought about the unusual way Xander acted when I first came into the kitchen this morning. I'd thought that maybe I was giving off some vibe that I'd woken up with a hard-on courtesy of the dream in which he had the leading role.

But that was just my own foolish paranoia. It was pretty obvious after the little coffee incident that Xander was still rattled from last night's attempt on his life. He'd seemed almost dazed, and a little confused, as he'd knelt on his floor mopping up the stain on his—no doubt expensive—rug. But after he'd talked it out and eaten some breakfast, everything had seemed to go back to normal.

Well, except that I couldn't seem to stop myself from checking in on him when I knew he wasn't looking. Or that was what I told myself I was doing every time I caught myself studying him from afar.

"He seems fine," I finally answered. "A little shaken, but that's to be expected."

"Right." Marcus pushed back from his desk and got to his feet, his broad shoulders testing the fabric of his suit jacket as he clasped his hands behind his back and made his way to his office's enormous window. "Another message came through the website last night. An email this time."

My spine stiffened, and when Marcus turned and pinned me with his grave eyes, I knew I wasn't going to like whatever he had to say.

"It appears your little ruse is working. A hit-and-run attempt and a ranting email all in one night? Seems your presence here has pissed this guy off. I hope you know what you're doing."

The blunt way in which he questioned my ability to do my job made me bristle. I didn't appreciate some stuffed shirt implying that I didn't know what I was doing. Especially when it came to looking after one of my own. The only reason I'd sat here this long was because the guy was footing the bill. Oh, and also because Xander had threatened my life if I did anything to get him fired.

"My plan *is* working, you're right," I said, getting to my feet. "We needed this creep to make himself known again. We needed a lead beyond a couple of threatening messages on a Twitter account, and it seems like we got it. I've been dealing with the scum of the earth a lot longer than you have, and trust me when I say I will put myself between it and Xander in a heartbeat. Can you say the same?"

Marcus was unflinching as he walked back to his desk and picked up a sheet of paper, which he held out to me. I went to take hold of it, and he didn't immediately let go, pinning me with calculating eyes.

"How do you know Alexander?"

"Excuse me?"

"Alexander. How do you know him?" The gaze that traveled over me was unreadable, as was the expression on his face. It was unnerving, but too bad for him: my nerves were like fucking steel. "When I told him to hire a bodyguard, he went directly to you. You're a cop, or so your background tells me—"

"I'm a detective," I said, wondering what the fuck he was getting at.

"Same thing."

"It's really not. I've got years of experience hunting down the worst of the worst under my belt, and I've been in situations that would make you shit your expensive business suits. So if you have a point to make, make it. Or give me the fucking letter."

Marcus didn't flinch, nor did his expression change. It was like he was carved out of stone. "My point is that I don't know you. *I* didn't vet you. So I want to know how Alexander knows you. It's obvious you're no stranger."

About done with his questions, I aimed my best *fuck you* look his way, channeling my inner Detective *Dick*, who I'd put on the back burner as of late.

"I don't see how that's any of your business." I yanked the paper out of Marcus's hand. "I'm here to do a job, and I'm doing it. So instead of questioning me, or acting like you think you're somehow superior, why don't you stay in your lane and I'll stay in mine? Now let me look at this latest email."

Marcus released the paper but remained silent.

ALEXANDER...WE need to talk.

Don't think I haven't seen the way you've been parading this new man of yours around under my nose. So fucking pleased with yourself, aren't you? That you've finally snagged a real *man. A* brave *man. One who jumps in front of cars for you...*

I bet a man like that is really good in bed too, huh? Strong, powerful—do you like that? Someone who takes control? Because you know what, Alexander? I can do that. And I bet I can do it better. Maybe you can tell me how I measure up when I tie you to my bed and fuck you right through it. Sound like a good plan? I think so.

I don't know why you had to go and make me compete for your affection like this. But I understand now, and I'm willing to do what it takes, because you're meant2bemine, and by the end of this you will be.

As I SCANNED the words twice over, nausea rolled in my gut. This crazy fucker was delusional, and the sooner I caught him, the better I'd feel about all this.

I folded up the message and looked to Marcus. "Is there anything else?"

Marcus briskly shook his head, and I turned on my heel and headed for the door. But just before I walked through it, I stopped and looked back at him.

"Oh, and one last thing. If you've got a problem with how I'm conducting this detail for Xander, get the fuck over it. Because I'm not going anywhere until this motherfucker is caught or rolled away in a body bag. Got it?"

24

XANDER

"SOOO, TELL ME about this sexy new guy you've been spotted canoodling with around the newsroom while I've been away. Ryan won't give me anything."

"*Canoodling?* I don't think so." I stared in the mirror at Cynthia, my hair and makeup stylist, and rolled my eyes. "You're back one day from your Tahitian vacation and you're already sniffing around for gossip. Why am I not surprised?"

"I have no idea. I'm more surprised that you were able to keep a secret this big and...*strong* away from me."

Big, strong, and sexy? Were we really describing Sean? But as I thought about the way he'd thrown himself in front of a car for me last night, and how he'd looked in my kitchen this morning in his sweats, those adjectives seemed frighteningly accurate.

"Hello, earth to Xander."

I shook my head. "I'm sorry, but I don't kiss and tell."

Cynthia laughed. "Since when? Were you, or were you not, the one who told me what a good kisser Benton Hale from ABC News was?"

I opened my mouth to deny her claim, but couldn't. "That was one time, and only because it was—"

"*Benton* Hale?"

"Shh," I said, and turned to look around her.

"Oh, relax and face the mirror. No one's in here, and you're on in twenty. I need that time to make you look good."

I aimed my most withering stare her way, and when she smiled sunnily, I groaned and slumped back in my chair.

Cynthia had been my stylist for as long as I could remember. She knew all my secrets—well, the ones I was willing to talk about—and I trusted her like a sister. She was smart, funny, and honest, and the fact that she could make me look good after being awake for twenty-four hours covering a monstrous hurricane down in the gulf made her invaluable to me.

She was a true friend, and the fact that I had to lie to her right now made me feel like a total shit.

"Now. You were telling me about..."

"Nothing?"

"No, that doesn't sound right. I believe you were telling me about Mr. Tall, Dark, and Dreamy, and whether or not you are going to be making this public on Saturday night at the NPF Awards. Now there's a man who would look *good* in a tux."

Oh shit, with everything that had been going on, I'd

completely forgotten about the award show. The National Press Foundation held it every year, and not once had I taken a date. But deciding to tackle the least difficult part of the conversation first, I said, "Can we please not call him that?"

"What? Mr. Tall, Dark, and Dreamy?"

"Yes. That."

"Oh, come on. He walked you up to work today. If that isn't dreamy, I don't know what is."

I bet she'd think it was much less dreamy if I told her Sean was here because Marcus had demanded a full brief on how we'd almost been run over last night. Oh, and the fact that he wasn't my boyfriend but my bodyguard, and the annoying older brother to my best friend who I'd known since I was a teenager.

Yes, all of that definitely made the fact that he'd escorted me up to my office much *less* dreamy. But since I couldn't actually say any of that, I plastered a smile on. "He *is* pretty amazing."

"I bet. I can't remember the last time you brought a guy around here."

Try never.

"Oh, except for Bailey. He was such a sweetheart."

"Still is."

"Well, yeah." She sighed as she powdered my face. "Such a shame that didn't work out. But at least the two of you are still friends."

"The best. I can't imagine my life without him in it." As

I reached for my coffee on the makeup counter and took a sip, Cynthia picked up the brush and blow dryer.

"And what's he think about Sean? Did he give him the stamp of approval yet?"

I choked on the coffee, a fit of coughs erupting as Cynthia eyed me in the mirror.

"You okay?"

I cleared my throat and nodded. "Uh-huh. Just went down the wrong way. But yes, Bailey definitely likes him. Loves him, actually." Which wasn't a lie. Bailey did love his brother.

"Whew. For a second there I thought there was going to be trouble in paradise. There's nothing worse than when the best friend disapproves of the boyfriend."

Cynthia switched on the blow dryer before I could answer, and I couldn't help but think how much Bailey would disapprove of the way I'd been feeling around his oldest brother lately.

Damn it. I hadn't been lying when I said I couldn't imagine my life without him in it, and I wasn't about to let my confused anatomy ruin a lifelong friendship.

Sean and I were just playing roles that neither of us enjoyed. He was here to help keep me safe. Nothing more, nothing less.

But as I stared at my reflection, I was honest enough to admit to myself that if that were really true, I wouldn't be imagining how good he would look in a tux. Not to mention just how vividly I could imagine him out of it.

25

SEAN

"WE NEED TO talk."

All evening, I'd been trying to decide the best way to approach Xander about the email Marcus had given me. I didn't want to worry him more, but he needed to know this creep had reached out again.

If anything, "meant2bemine" seemed more determined than ever. Not to mention more pissed off.

"In my experience, nothing good ever comes after those four words. So do you mind if I get a glass of wine first?" Xander tossed his wallet and phone onto the kitchen counter and headed for the fridge.

"Sure thing," I said, watching him go, and my eyes caught on the perfectly tailored cut of the charcoal suit he'd worn home tonight, and just how well it outlined his frame.

Okay, the fact that I was noticing his changing habits and just how well his suit fit him made my palms sweat a little. Since when did I pay attention to shit like clothes and complementary colors?

"I notice you're not correcting me on the 'nothing good ever comes after that' bit," Xander said as he grabbed a bottle of wine from the door.

Still caught up in my head, I ignored what he said. "Uh, you got a beer in there?"

Xander arched a brow, but then he nodded and leaned in to grab a Stella Artois.

"You want something to eat?" he asked as he slid it across the counter.

"Nah, I'm good. But if you want something, go ahead."

Xander took a wine glass from one of the cabinets. "I had a quick bite at the station, but I know you didn't, so..."

"I'm okay, Xander. Just get what you need and then we'll chat."

Xander slowly pulled the cork out of the bottle, his curiosity obvious. But that'd be cleared up soon enough.

I looked to his living room, and then the doors that led out to the balcony. Maybe it'd be better to give him this news outside. I didn't want to taint his home by allowing this asshole entrance—even if only through a letter.

"How about we go and sit on the balcony?"

"The terrace."

I shrugged. "Same thing."

"They're not, actually," Xander said as he walked toward the double doors leading outside. "A balcony is usually a small space situated off a portion of the upper floor. Whereas a terrace is a patio, or full living space attached to the outside of a building. Hence, a rooftop terrace."

As the doors shut behind us, Xander turned to see me standing just outside the door.

"You don't really care about any of that, do you?"

"Not really. But I'm getting used to you schooling me in my lack of knowledge when it comes to you and your upper-class ways."

"That's not what I was—" Xander sighed. "Sorry. I didn't mean to lecture you."

I smirked and took a swig of beer before walking over to him. "It's okay. I'm getting used to that too."

"My upper-class ways?"

"The lectures."

Xander grimaced and stared out at his multimillion-dollar view of Lake Michigan. "I don't know why I do that with you. I don't with anyone else."

"Lecture them?"

"Yes. What does it matter if you call it a balcony or a terrace? I knew what you meant."

"I don't know. Maybe you just like the fight?"

"The fight?"

"Yeah." I rested my arms on the thick stone rail that surrounded the entire upper floor of the building. "You know that if you poke at me I won't just roll over and agree with you. Maybe you like that. Someone giving you a run for your money."

"That's ridiculous." Xander screwed his nose up. "Who likes fighting with people?"

My lips twitched. "You do. You constantly fight with me."

"No, I—" Xander stopped himself from doing just that. As his eyes roved over my face, I wondered what exactly he saw now when he looked at me.

Bailey's brother? His unwanted bodyguard? Or the man he'd had to put up with most of his life and now found himself stuck with?

But before I did something stupid like *ask*, Xander said, "You wanted to talk to me?"

I nodded, set my beer down on the flat surface of the railing, and reached into my pocket.

As I pulled out the folded paper, Xander straightened. "What's that?"

"An email." I looked him in the eye, knowing I needed to be direct with this. No sugarcoating. Xander needed to know what was going on, and I needed to be honest with him. "It's from the same guy, meant2bemine. Marcus gave it to me this afternoon. It looks like our plan worked."

"*Your* plan," Xander said.

"Yes, my plan. He saw us together—several times would be my guess. But he wrote and sent this last night. Seems he doesn't like the competition."

Xander brought his glass to his lips, seeming to need the liquid courage, and then licked his lower lip. The action caused a stirring in my gut, and I took a step toward him.

Xander looked me in the eye, and the courage and bravery I saw made my admiration for him grow tenfold.

"What does it say?" Xander pointed to my hand. "The email. It's bad, isn't it?"

I ran my fingers across the top of the paper and nodded. There was no easy way to say it, no chance of making the words any less threatening or disgusting. So I held the paper out to him, and when Xander took it, I watched him closely, gauging his response.

It wasn't easy. Xander had one hell of a poker face. As his eyes followed the words from left to right down the page, blood began to pound in my ears.

"Xander?"

He said nothing, just stared at the email, and if it hadn't been for the slight tremble in his hand, I wouldn't have thought he was affected.

"Xander?" When he still didn't look up, I reached for his wrist, and he flinched away from me. "Hey," I said, holding my hands up. "It's okay."

"This..." Xander licked his lip, a habit I now recognized as nervous. "This is very...personal."

I slowly nodded. "It is."

"What he says here..." He turned the page around and pointed to the line. But I already knew which one he meant. "About tying me to the bed and, um, and—"

"I know what it says," I said. "He's just trying to scare you."

"It's working." Xander's fingers tightened on the paper, and he turned away, bracing himself with his other hand on the rail. "God, Sean."

He took in a deep breath and then let it out. "I've been

trying not to stress about this and become a paranoid nutcase who jumps at every single sound. But I have to tell you, it's getting harder and harder every day."

"I know." I carefully moved alongside him and studied his profile. With the breeze ruffling his thick hair across his forehead, I took in the straight line of his nose, his full lips, the stubble lining his prominent jaw line, and felt my cock jerk.

Shit, what was going on with me? Xander was dealing with some fucking psycho, and I was standing here, what? Checking him out?

Jesus. I mean, I'd always had a healthy sex drive. It was a great way to relieve some of the tension after weeks on a case. But never in all those years had I gotten caught up and distracted by a man. And definitely not Xander—

"There's an award ceremony this weekend."

As Xander's voice cut through my confused thoughts, I refocused on the email in his hand. Anywhere but on his face, the face I'd grown up looking at. The face that I'd never thought twice about until now...apparently.

"There is?"

"Yes. The NPF Awards, National Press Foundation. It's held every year. There's dinner and a ceremony."

"Huh," I brilliantly responded as I tried to pull my shit together. "I didn't know that."

"Why would you?"

"I don't know. I know about the Oscars and stuff."

"Weren't you the one who told me I wasn't quite *that* famous?"

"Yeah, I suppose I was." I flashed a crooked smile, satisfied my brain was back on track—for now. "But I've discovered over the last week or so that in the news world, you're basically Tom Cruise-level famous. Lemme guess, you're up for an award, right?"

"Three, actually. I was told last month and completely forgot about it until today, when someone mentioned it. I'm sorry."

"Hey, it's okay. You've had a lot going on, and you're telling me now." I rubbed my chin as I thought over a few things. "I am going to need you to tell me everything you know about the event, though, and who's running it. That way I can get into contact with them today or tomorrow and see if I can get another guy to come help out."

"God. I fucking hate this."

"Anyone in your situation would. This guy's disrupting your life."

"No," Xander whispered, his eyes filled with an emotion I'd never seen before—terror. "I don't care about that, not anymore. What I can't stand is how scared I am. I'm scared of my own damn shadow these days, Sean. And I hate that he has that power. I *hate* that I'm giving it to him."

26

XANDER

NEVER IN ALL my life had I felt so exposed, so open, and not because I was standing outside with nothing surrounding me but the rest of Chicago's high rises. All because some asshole had invaded my life, my mind, and I wasn't sure I'd ever be able to get him out.

"You're not *giving* it to him," Sean said, and though I wanted to believe him, I found it difficult.

"No? Then why do I want to lock myself in my bedroom and not come out until he's caught? I feel like a fucking coward."

Sean reached for my arm and turned me toward him, and I realized just how close we were.

"*You* are not a coward."

I averted my gaze, not wanting to see what he really thought lingering on his face. Sean took my chin between his fingers and turned my face to him, and I sucked in a breath.

There was no judgment in his dark blue eyes, no disapproval, just a bone-deep concern that I found difficult to fight.

"You're dealing with a situation that most people will never even have to think about in their life. And as the person who's usually called to investigate the horrendous ending to that kind of thing, your impulse to lock yourself in your bedroom isn't all that shocking. If I had my way, I'd lock you in there myself."

While I knew he meant that regarding keeping me safe from the lunatic chasing me, my stomach flipped at the idea of being locked in my bedroom with Sean.

I swayed in closer to him, the feel of his fingers touching my skin, and his eyes that were promising to keep me safe from danger all making me want to put my life in his hands —and maybe some other parts of myself too.

"That doesn't seem very smart, locking myself away," I finally said. "We have no idea how long I'd be there. We don't even know who this person is."

"I wouldn't care." Sean's fingers tightened a fraction, and that slight pressure against my jaw made my heart thump. "You'd be safe."

This was dangerous. Not just the threat against my life, but what Sean was doing to my peace of mind. My breath caught at the fierce determination behind his words, and when I slicked my tongue across my bottom lip and his eyes fell to the move, warning signs began to flash before my eyes.

This—what I was feeling—wasn't real. It was just a response to feeling so alone, so vulnerable, and I needed to remember that. Just as I needed to remember that *Sean* was straight. Straight and so completely *not* who I needed to go to for comfort at a time like this. He didn't even realize what he was doing to me right now, the way his attention was bringing to life emotions that would never have seen the light of day if it hadn't been for this specific set of circumstances. *Right?*

"Sean..."

"Hmm?"

I reached up and circled his wrist, and as soon as my fingers touched his skin, he jolted as though I'd shocked him, and we both dropped our hands. "I don't think barricading myself in my bedroom is going to stop him, do you?"

Sean blinked as though trying to clear his head, and I understood the sudden confusion. If he was experiencing anything remotely like what I was, then his brain was firing off nonsensical notions that were clouding his reality.

"Sean?"

"Sorry," he said, and cleared his throat. "No. I don't think so. He's fixated."

I nodded. "Right. So for now we...?"

Sean rubbed his fingers over his lips, and I found myself watching the move much more closely than I would have a month ago, a week ago. Hell, a couple of days ago.

"We keep doing what we're doing. We're clearly getting to him. He believes the act and is infuriated by it, which means he's more likely to fuck up and give us a better chance of locating him."

Well, that sounded…terrifying. "I don't know if I can do that."

"You can. I know you can. And I'm going to be right there with you the entire time. I'm not going to let anything happen to you."

I swallowed, my throat suddenly dry. "Okay."

"Okay." Sean ran a hand through his hair and then leaned against the rail. "So, uh, about this award thingy. How fancy is it?"

"How fancy?"

"Yeah. You said it's dinner and a ceremony, so I figure it's pretty uppity, huh?"

Oh yeah. I grimaced, knowing he wouldn't like the answer to this. "It's black tie."

"A tux?" Sean groaned. "Of course it's a fucking tux."

I wasn't sure if it was the culmination of such a messed-up week or Sean's put-out tone, but my lips twitched at his predictable response.

"What?"

"Nothing."

"Uh-huh, because that smirk on your face really screams 'nothing.'"

"I was just wondering if you've ever worn a tux before, that's all."

"That would be a no. Where would I ever wear a tux?"

"An award ceremony, I hope."

"Yeah, yeah, don't stress over there. I promise not to show up looking like I'm going to a frat house kegger."

"A frat house kegger? Now, that sounds classy."

"What can I say? I'm a classy guy."

When I just stared at him, Sean laughed.

"Relax. If worse comes to worst, I'll get your assistant Ryan to hook me up. He likes me. I'm sure he'd be happy to help."

He wasn't wrong. Ryan had taken a shine to him. It was strange, but up until this little charade, I'd only ever been around people who had a preconceived idea of who Sean was. So to see someone so taken by his gruff kind of charm was...interesting, to say the least.

"I won't let you miss your big award night." Sean reached for his beer, and as he brought it to his lips, I headed toward the doors, ready to get inside and go to bed.

At the last second, though, I stopped and turned to give him back the email and nearly ran into Sean.

"Shit, sorry," he said as he reached for me and I righted myself.

"That's okay." My voice sounded odd, breathy, as I stared up at the man I'd argued with more times than I could remember, and my world once again shifted, as did his place in it. "Sean?"

"Yeah."

"I think you should let me go."

Sean's eyes roved over my face, and as I held my breath, waiting for him to realize what was going on and shove me away, he drew me closer.

"Sean..." I placed a hand on his chest and stared up at his blazing eyes.

This was insanity. But as the wind whipped up and

ruffled his hair across his forehead, I wanted nothing more than to move up to my toes and brush my lips over his.

"Let me go," I said again, the suggestion a whisper on the wind, and when Sean released me, I handed him the letter and took a step back. "Good night."

Sean looked down to the paper. "Yeah, night."

I disappeared inside and hightailed it to my room, deciding that barricading myself in there for the next however many hours didn't seem like the dumbest idea after all.

27

XANDER

THE STEADY BEAT of Fall Out Boy blared through my headphones the following morning as my feet pounded against the belt of the treadmill. I was coming up to the final mile in my workout, and as I cut my eyes to the opposite side of my indoor pool area where Sean was lounged back watching the TV, I tried to block out the weird tension that had settled between us since last night.

After that moment out on the terrace, we'd both reverted to our usual roles and kept our fake relationship safely in a box for now, since there was no one else around.

That was fine by me. I was walking on eggshells already as it was. As my workout came to a close, it didn't escape my notice that I couldn't even enjoy a couple hours in here without thinking about the shitstorm that was now my life. At this rate, I was going to drive myself mad.

As I hit stop on the machine and the belt slowed, I grabbed my water bottle and drained the contents. I wiped off my brow and slung the towel around the back of my neck. I glanced over to the lounge and saw Sean getting to his feet, his eyes locked on me.

A shiver of awareness raced down my spine, and I was cognizant that that was one of the reasons for the tension between us.

Somewhere between Sean moving in and taking on the role of my fake boyfriend to now, I'd begun responding to him as though we were going to end up in one of the nine beds in this house, and I had a horrible suspicion that I'd somehow projected my feelings onto him.

There was no way in hell that Sean Bailey would have ever eyed my mouth the way he had last night—like he wanted to take a nice, long taste of it—and there was no way before the last two weeks that I would have ever wanted him to. But this forced confinement was making the two of us act in ways we never would've before, and if we didn't pull it together soon, life would become incredibly difficult—not to mention frustrating as hell.

It was time to man up. Time to be an adult about things and to stop thinking about being in such close confines with a man who was making my hormones go haywire.

But as Sean walked around the end of the pool, I found myself studying his sure, confident stride. There wasn't one hint of hesitation as he made his way to me, and as he came up my side of the pool to the treadmill and weights, any thought other than how damn sexy he looked left my mind. I was in so much fucking trouble.

"Good run?" he said.

"Yeah, it wasn't bad." I wiped at my face again, deciding if a towel was covering my eyes it might help—but it didn't.

"I was wondering if you'd mind me going for a swim this morning? I won't take long, 'bout twenty minutes?"

A swim? But wouldn't that mean—

Sean peeled his shirt off, revealing his muscular torso, and I almost swallowed my tongue.

"I wore my board shorts and thought you could just sit over there and wait for me until I'm done." He tossed his shirt by my feet, and for a second, I wondered if he was doing this on purpose. "That okay with you?"

Was what okay? I'd forgotten what the hell we were talking about.

"Xander? You all right?"

No. No, I was not. And it was obvious from the look on his face that Sean had no clue what the hell he was doing to me. "I, um... I'm just feeling a little lightheaded after my run, that's all."

Sean took a step toward me, and I backed up and reached for the treadmill, feigning dizziness to cover up that I wanted to lean in and touch all of that toned skin.

Who knew Sean was hiding such a body under those horrible suits?

"Maybe you should go grab yourself a Gatorade real quick? Or some crackers. I don't want you to pass out on me."

I nodded. "I think that's a good idea."

"Okay. But don't be long," Sean said as I walked by him,

making sure to take a wide berth. "Ten minutes max or I'm coming to get you."

I all but ran from the pool area. With Sean standing that close to me and that...well, naked, I wasn't sure I could be held responsible for my actions. After all, I'd almost kissed the guy just last night, and he'd been fully dressed then.

I booked it down the hall toward the kitchen, not to grab a Gatorade but because it was the room farthest from the pool. Just as I was passing the elevator, the intercom chimed, indicating the front desk was calling.

Frowning, I hit the call button. "Marvin? Hi."

"Oh, hello, Xander. How are you this morning?"

"I'm good. Was there something you needed?" Sean had been very clear with management that under no circumstances were anyone other than Marvin and Gina—the two front desk clerks who had been fully checked out—allowed to call up to my apartment.

"No, nothing I need. But a flower delivery was just dropped off for you."

"Really?"

"Yes, sir. A very fancy one."

Ah, okay. I knew what that was for: the awards. Marcus always sent flowers to his nominated employees—or Carmen did—and, deciding there was no harm with Marvin bringing them up, I gave him the go-ahead and waited for him to arrive.

Minutes later, the doors slid open, and a huge bouquet of crimson roses close to filled the elevator. Marvin, an older gentlemen, peered around the blooms and offered me a wide smile.

"Stunning, aren't they?" he said as he handed them over. "Is it a special occasion?"

They definitely were beautiful. Flawlessly cut and displayed, they were classy, elegant, and absolutely gorgeous.

"I was nominated for an award at work."

Marvin whistled. "Must be some award. There's a note right here." He plucked it out of the back of the stems, handed it over, and got back inside the elevator. "Enjoy them. That's one of the most beautiful bouquets I've ever seen."

As the doors closed and I placed the vase on the entry table, I noticed how heavy it was.

I opened the note, drew the card out, and felt all the blood drain from my face.

FOR YOUR COLLECTION.
I told you I knew you.
You're meanttobemine.

MY HANDS SHOOK as I read the words over and over again, and when my vision began to blur, I reached for the wall to steady myself and heard Sean calling my name from down the hall.

I took in several gulps of air and looked at the huge

bouquet in front of me, trying to discern what exactly was going on, and that was when I spotted it: the insignia in the vase.

Baccarat. Wow... How had he known that I collected that crystal?

It was no secret where I lived. Being in the public eye took away that privilege, and we already knew that this slimeball knew my address—he'd flat-out told us he did in the first messages he'd sent.

But how had he known about the crystal? That I had several items in my office from their collection, along with the chandelier hanging in my great room?

My stomach twisted into a vicious knot as my fingers tightened around the card until my nails nearly broke the skin of my palm. I needed to get back to the pool to show Sean what I was holding. But first, I needed to work out how to stop my head from spinning, because I was in real danger of passing out now that I knew *meanttobemine* had somehow seen the inside of my place.

28

SEAN

XANDER HAD BEEN gone too long.

I touched the end of the pool wall and raised my head to look at the door he'd disappeared out of nearly fifteen minutes ago, then tore my goggles off and tossed them up onto the tiled edge.

Fifteen minutes wasn't long in the scheme of things. But when it came to him being out of sight and out of earshot, I didn't like it—whether it was in his fortress or not.

I ran my hands through my hair and tried not to think about the real reason I'd needed to go for a swim. But every time I tried to shove aside this new obsession with watching Xander's every move, my mind rewound to last night, when I'd been two seconds away from discovering if his mouth felt as soft as it looked.

Fuck. What the hell am I doing? This was Xander, for fuck's sake, a man. But that didn't seem to matter anymore, because the second he was close, my eyes found him, my body came alive, and my cock ached in a way that it hadn't in years.

I was confused and frustrated, and trying my fucking hardest to act like everything was fine and dandy. But this gig was getting harder by the second.

Yeah, okay, maybe don't think of it like that.

I looked at the clock on the wall and cursed before I called out Xander's name. The pool was at the far end of the house, but with no other noise in the place, he should be able to hear me and respond. When there was nothing, I shoved off the wall and headed for the stairs. I was done with this "waiting for him to grab a snack" bullshit.

I climbed out of the pool and was about to grab my towel when I heard the door open, and turned to see Xander.

"'Bout time you got back. I was about to send out a search..." My words trailed off as I looked him over, wondering why he'd frozen just inside the door. But as I took in his pale face, grim expression, and the clenched fist by his side, the hairs on the back of my neck stood tall.

Uncaring of my dripping shorts, I was over to him before I took my next breath. "What happened?"

Xander swallowed, his usually vibrant eyes glazed over as though he were in a state of shock. When he didn't answer, I looked him over, trying to assess if he was hurt in any way.

"Xander?" When he blinked, I shook him a little, hoping to shock him out of whatever state it was he was in. "Xander? What happened?"

When he moved his right arm, I quickly let it go,

thinking I might've been hurting him—but then I saw it. A small, crumpled card in his hand.

"What's that?"

Xander's jaw bunched as he held it out to me. "It...it came with some roses. Just a few minutes ago."

"Just a few— You let someone in the *house*?" I barked, and Xander flinched. "What were you thinking?" A wave of panic turned my vision red, and when Xander didn't answer, I tightened my grip on his arm. "What the fuck were you thinking?"

"I *wasn't*, okay?" Xander shouted. "Marvin called up, and I thought the flowers were from Marcus, and...I didn't think. And can you please stop cursing at me? I'm already stressed enough as it is. I don't really need Detective Dick right now. I need Sean."

As Xander began to tremble, I told myself to take a deep breath and calm the hell down. He was right, and I was ashamed that I'd let my alarm cloud my judgment.

I let go and crossed my arms over my chest, then realized I was still in nothing but a pair of wet swim shorts.

Not about to excuse myself for a quick change of clothes, I shoved aside my lack of attire and said, "Look, I'm sorry I yelled at you. I'm just pissed off that this fucker got to you here. Inside your house."

Xander said nothing as I looked down at his trembling hand, and my annoyance vanished. He was shaken to his very core. I reached for the small card he held then unfolded the note, more aware than ever that this piece of shit had just upped the ante.

I clenched my hand around the note as I ground my molars together, and then I read the words over. "For your collection? What is he talking about?"

"The vase. He sent the roses in a—" Xander covered his mouth, and knowing I needed to re-establish the trust I'd just stomped all over, I reached for his hand.

Xander flinched, but when I curled my fingers around his, he held on tight.

"He sent them in a what?" I asked.

"A Baccarat vase." When I narrowed my eyes, confused over the significance, he whispered, "I collect Baccarat crystal. The only people who would know that are people who have been in my office at work, or here in my house."

Motherfucker. The reality of just how dangerous this asshole was had never been clearer now that he had penetrated Xander's sanctuary.

"Where are the roses?"

"In the foyer."

"Okay. Leave them there. I need to look at them. You said Marvin brought them up?"

"Yes. But he's just a sweet old man. You know that—"

"It doesn't matter who he is, Xander. I still need to talk to him."

"I know. I know."

I let go of his hand and ran my fingers through my wet hair. "I'm going to go and get changed. I'd prefer if you waited—"

"I'll be in my bedroom." I studied him for a second, and then Xander added, "I think I'm going to call Marcus and let him know to bring David in for tonight's broadcast. I need to lie down for a while. This is too much, Sean. This is all…" His voice shook and then cracked. "It's too much."

I nodded, knowing that was the best plan. Then I snatched up a towel from a rack in the room and took the crook of his arm, guiding him down the hall to his bedroom.

Once he was safely tucked away, I headed to my room with one thing on my mind: tracking down this chickenshit and putting an end to this sick and twisted game he was playing.

29

XANDER

THE SOUND OF my bedroom door closing seemed as loud as a gunshot as I shut myself behind the thick wooden doors and prayed for silence. But as I stood there with my fingers tight around the handle and my legs unmoving, I was aware that while I may be able to shut the door on the world outside, the one thing I couldn't escape was my mind.

I shut my eyes and took in a deep breath, and as I let it out, I tried to banish from it the roses, the email, and the hit-and-run. But it was no use, and as it all began to spiral out of control, my legs began to shake, and I had to lean into the door to keep myself upright.

Who was doing this to me? And why? Had I somehow done something to provoke this person? I didn't think so. But as each day passed and the advances became more brazen, more personal, I was finding it difficult to brush this off as some overly enthusiastic fan.

Whoever this was wanted contact. They wanted me.

And if they couldn't have me, it seemed my blood would suffice. I wasn't sure what to do with that.

When I was fairly certain my legs wouldn't give out from under me, I let go of the handle and made myself cross to the bathroom to have a quick shower. I kicked off my sneakers and quickly stripped, and as I turned the spray on and the warm water found me, I stepped under it and closed my eyes.

Breathe in... Breathe out... Keep yourself upright.

The last thing I needed was to have a panic attack and pass out. Sean was currently downstairs trying to find out what he could about the delivery, and I'd rather he didn't come back to find me naked and unconscious on my tile floor.

And speaking of Sean, he was a whole other problem I hadn't been prepared for. An unexpected problem who was saying all the right things at all the right times, and making me feel a way that I hadn't in a long time.

I tipped my face up into the spray and tried to push aside the gentle way he'd comforted me last night. The unfailing way he'd assured me that nothing would hurt me while I was under his protection. I also tried to forget the image of his strong body that had been on full display in my pool earlier. But as my shaft stiffened in response to that very clear visual, I knew I was losing that battle.

For days now, I'd been trying to convince myself that maybe my body was just confused. That maybe I was stressed and worried and Sean was someone I knew I could trust, and that was why he was starting to look like a viable option.

But I knew that wasn't true. *Viable* wasn't the right word here. But the other option scared me, because thinking of Sean as the *only* option who could appease this ache was foolhardy in every way imaginable.

Things had shifted between us. I hadn't been prepared for that. And as the days and nights passed, it wasn't going away. If anything, it was intensifying, and the more time we spent around one another, the more I thought I saw a flicker of...what? Interest from Sean? That seemed highly unlikely, and yet that niggling feeling remained.

I stepped out of the shower, quickly dried off, and listened to see if I could hear any other sounds throughout the house indicating Sean was back.

When all that greeted me was silence, my stomach twisted around on itself, my anxiety now at an all-time high.

Heading out to my bed, I grabbed my phone to see a weather alert for tomorrow—*Warning: Extreme Heat Advisory*—and groaned at the idea of the first scorcher to hit Chicago for the summer. It'd been getting hotter every day for sure, but it sounded like tomorrow was going to be the beginning of the extreme.

After clearing it from the screen, I sent off a quick text to Marcus to call in David for the night, then I grabbed the bottle of melatonin from my bedside drawer, determined to put any thoughts other than sleep out of my mind. I crawled beneath my covers and lay there staring at my ceiling, thinking that maybe a few hours of shuteye would help clear my head.

Maybe that would help put things back where they belonged with Sean, because right now, as my world was spinning out of control, the only thing that made any sense was how safe I felt when he was near, and just how much I wanted him back by my side as soon as humanly possible.

30

SEAN

MY MOOD WAS a dark cloud surrounding me as I marched down the hall toward the elevator. I was fuming mad, and having no one to take it out on, I punched the button with a little more force than necessary, wanting to get downstairs as soon as possible.

The doors slid open and I stepped inside, and as I rounded back to hit the lobby button, I caught sight of the roses that sat on the foyer table and my vision turned a similar shade of red.

When I finally caught up with this motherfucker, he was gonna want to either be dead or unconscious, because I was just about done with this brand of bullshit.

I stared at my blurry reflection in the doors as the elevator began its descent. I'd changed over the last couple of weeks with this new haircut, new clothes, and new perspective on the man who lived in this uptown castle.

But one thing that hadn't changed was my attitude, my

determination to see this shithead hunting Xander brought down, and to do that, several things needed to happen.

First, I needed to calm down. That was easier said than done, however, because every time I thought about the panic I'd seen on Xander's face, I wanted to slam my fist through the nearest wall.

Second, I needed to find out who had dropped those fucking flowers off.

When the elevator doors opened, I stepped out and scanned the immediate area. I'd spoken to the building's manager, Gerald, when I moved in, and he'd assured me that there were working surveillance cameras in the parking garage, lobby, and all elevators. As I crossed the marble floors, beelining it to the front desk, my eyes shifted from each of the corner cameras and I made a mental note to be sure to ask for each of those videos.

"Hello, sir. What can I do for you today?" Marvin said with a bright smile as I approached the desk, but when he caught sight of my stoic expression, his smile faltered.

"Yeah, hi. I'd like to speak to you, if you have a minute."

Marvin frowned, his big, bushy eyebrows all but colliding on his forehead. "Uh, of course. You're staying with Xander, aren't you?"

I narrowed my eyes, wondering just how much Gerald had informed his staff about the reason I was here. If he wanted to keep his job, he would've told them jack fucking shit.

"That's right. And you delivered some flowers to him around twenty minutes ago. Is that right?"

It was clear Marvin was aware there were new rules when it came to the top tenant in the building, just not all the finer details as to why.

"Yes. That's right. But I called up to let him know he had a delivery. It wasn't until Xander told me to bring them up that I did."

Shit. That went hand in hand with the story Xander had given me. So he hadn't been covering for the old guy. I was really going to have to get through to him just how important it was that he not trust anyone—not even Marvin. I didn't care if he won the fucking lottery and they dropped by to bring him a check. No one was going to set foot in Xander's apartment again until this was all over. Not unless they went through me.

Schooling my temper the best I could, I lowered my voice to a much more congenial tone. "That's okay. They were just so, um, nice, and Xander wanted me to ask if you remembered anything about the person who delivered them. He wanted to call the florist and leave a tip."

"Oh, of course." Marvin again flashed that bright smile. "Let me see. He was a young man and very nice. Tall... maybe your height? He was thin but wore sunglasses and a cap, so I can't tell you much about his hair. But he was clean-shaven."

"How young?"

Marvin chuckled. "Everyone feels young to me."

"If you had to guess?"

"Hmm, late twenties, maybe? Thirty?"

I tapped my finger on the front desk and then glanced

behind me, checking out the empty lobby. I really needed to see the surveillance video. "Would you be able to tell me if Gerald is here?" When Marvin's eyes widened in alarm, I added, "I just remembered he asked me to come down and sign some paperwork, and I might as well kill two birds with one stone."

"Ah, I see. Let me call and check if he's in his office."

As Marvin stepped away, I turned around and leaned back against the desk. I wanted to see this guy that had delivered the flowers. It could just be someone who worked for the florist, I supposed, and I'd be sure to follow up with that. But sometimes these assholes got cocky. Sometimes they wanted to get closer to their infatuation and took risks, and I wasn't about to leave without at least checking it out.

"You're in luck, he's here. He said to go on back. His office is through that door over there, and—"

"I remember. I met with him when I moved in."

Marvin gave a brisk nod, and I headed across the lobby and pushed through the side door, making my way down to where Gerald was standing in his open doorway.

"Detective Bailey."

"Gerald," I said as I stepped inside his cramped office and he shut the door behind me.

"What can I do for you?" As he took a seat behind his desk, I remained standing, not about to get comfortable when I wanted to track down the cameras and look at them—now.

"You can get me this morning's surveillance video."

"Why? Did something happen?"

"Yes. One of your employees brought a flower delivery up to Xander's this morning." Gerald's mouth fell open, and I nodded. "So I'm going to ask you again. Can you get me that video?"

He all but jumped to his feet. "Yes, yes, of course. I'm so sorry this happened. I told Marvin not to—"

"It doesn't matter who it was," I said, suddenly feeling protective over the old man for Xander's sake. He might've fucked up, yeah. But I didn't want the guy fired. "I just want to look at the video."

"Yes. I understand. Come with me." Gerald rushed to the door and pulled it open. I followed him outside, and as we entered a small room full of electrical equipment and several TV monitors, I finally felt like I was getting somewhere.

He sat down behind the controls, and I moved in behind him, pointing to the monitors surveying the lobby, and one which was aimed at the desk.

"There, those four, but that one in particular. Can you rewind it? About thirty minutes ago?"

Gerald pushed a button and nothing happened. "What in the...?"

"What's wrong?" I said.

"It's not rewinding."

"The feed?"

"Yes." Gerald moved to the wall of equipment behind me and opened up the door, then he shook his head. "I don't understand."

"What?"

Gerald looked back at me, a frown deeply etched between his brows.

"*What?*"

"The drive is gone. There's nothing in here. There's nothing recording. All you're seeing is a live feed. That's why I can't rewind it."

I fucking knew it. That ballsy motherfucker had been inside the building and had been smart enough to take the one thing that would've proven it.

But how had he known where to go to get the drive?

"Don't you have a backup?" I demanded, my annoyance boiling up inside me now that I knew he'd been so close and yet he'd somehow managed to slip away—again.

"No, we don't."

"And there's no lock on this door. Fucking perfect." Incompetence at its finest. "What about a camera on the hall back here?"

"We have one, yes. But all the feeds for the day would've been stored on that drive."

Fuck! Just when I thought I would have a strong, decent lead, maybe a face, I had nothing. This was great, just fucking great. If I could get a break sometime soon, that would be amazing.

"I don't want anyone calling up to, or coming into, Xander's place until I tell you otherwise," I barked. "Do you understand?"

"Yes, of course."

"And for fuck's sake, buy a new tape or drive or whatever the fuck this asshole stole back in there, just in case he comes back." I pulled open the door, and as it slammed against the wall, I stormed out of the security room muttering, "Motherfucker."

BY THE TIME I stepped off the elevator into Xander's place, I'd made sure I'd calmed down. It wouldn't do him any good to see me in a rage, and the last thing I wanted to do was spook him further.

In fact, I was hoping he was knocked out cold and was getting a bit of rest. That way I could take a second to process all of this and decide what to do next.

The florist was at the top of the list. I wanted to call them up and check to see if anyone worked for them that matched the description Marvin had given me. If that was a no, then I wanted to know who called the order in and who came to pick it up. If I could get an answer on either one of those things, I had a feeling I'd finally get somewhere.

But first things first: I needed to check on Xander. As I made my way down the hall, I was hyperaware of just how quiet it was up here. Not a sound could be heard throughout the house, and that gave me hope he was currently visiting la-la land.

I stopped outside his door and softly knocked, and when there was no response, I decided there was no harm in checking to make sure he was safely tucked in bed.

I pushed open the door a crack and looked inside, and just as I made out his form beneath the covers, Xander sat up and looked my way.

"Hey," he said, his voice a little drowsy from napping, and just as I was about to tell him I'd come back later, Xander added, "Come in."

"Are you sure?" I asked, but found myself stepping inside and shutting the door. "I just wanted to check on you, but you should rest."

Xander gave a tight smile and then rubbed a hand over his weary face. "It's okay. I'm finding it hard to drift off. Too much going on up here." He tapped the side of his head. "Did you find out anything?"

I heard the question, I knew I did. But my eyes had fallen to all the naked skin on display, as he sat there with a sheet draped across his lap.

"Sean?"

"Huh?" My eyes flew back to his.

"Did you find out anything?"

I grimaced. "We can talk about that—"

"Now, Sean. I want to talk about it now."

"Okay." I walked across the room to stand at the foot of his bed, and I would've been lying if I'd said that seeing him there didn't make my palms sweat and my pulse beat a little faster. "The hard drive is gone."

Xander stared at me blankly, and I shoved my hands in the pockets of my jeans in case they did something stupid like start to shake.

Shit. Here he was trying to get serious information out of me, and all I could focus on was how good he looked half-naked and sleep-sexy.

Focus, Sean. Focus. "The security system for the hotel

uses hard drives to record the video. It stores up to a month's worth of footage. The one that would've had today's video? It's gone."

"Gone? I...I don't understand. What do you mean gone? Isn't the room where it's kept monitored or something?"

"Not very fucking well. It seems whoever this fucker is knew how, or when, he could get back there with no one noticing."

"So this guy is smart? Great."

Xander shoved back the covers and swung his legs over the edge of the bed, and I was more than a little relieved that he was wearing those loose grey pants.

"I felt slightly better thinking he was just some crackpot with a fixation. But he's *smart*, Sean. He's dismantling surveillance videos now?"

Xander shot to his feet, and as he did he lost his balance, because he started to pitch forward. Before I could think twice about it, I was around the mattress and up the two stairs of the platform bed reaching for him.

"Whoa, careful there." As Xander clutched at my arms and steadied himself, he looked up into my eyes, and the worry there made my heart ache for him. "You listen to me. I want you to get back in bed, close your eyes, and forget about this for a few more hours."

"But—"

"Shh." I pressed a finger against his lips. "You already called Marcus, I assume?"

Xander nodded.

"Good. Then I want you to get back in bed and rest. When was the last time you got a really good sleep?"

Xander blinked, and when I lowered my hand, he said, "The night before I turned up on your doorstep."

I chuckled. "I'm going to try to not take that too personally."

Xander tried for a half-smile, but failed.

"You're exhausted. Get in bed, Xander."

As I continued to hold on to him, Xander stared up at me with an expression I couldn't quite decipher, then he straightened, and I let him go.

"I'm going to go and sit over there by your cozy fireplace and keep an eye on you, okay?"

"Okay."

As I walked over to his seating area, I could feel his eyes on me almost as vividly as his hands had just been. I took a seat and stretched my legs out in front of me. As I watched him climb back into bed, I had the intense desire to lie down beside him.

Instead of doing that, however, I watched Xander turn to his side, prop his hands up under his cheek, and level his eyes on me, as he drifted back off to sleep and left me sitting there with about a hundred and one questions as to why I suddenly wanted to hold him instead of watch over him from afar.

31

XANDER

MY FEET SLAPPED *against the pavement and my heart pounded out an accompanying rhythm as I ran full speed down the road. The sun had just set, and as the night closed in, all signs of life vanished from sight.*

With my legs pumping and my chest heaving, I glanced over my shoulder, searching for that which was chasing me. But as I scanned the shadows for the one causing such panic, all I saw was a vast void.

That couldn't be right. There was something back there, something hunting me. But as my eyes strained against the never-ending stretch of darkness that seemed to be closing in, I felt my terror intensify.

Run, *my mind chanted.* Run, *and don't stop.*

And just as I turned to bolt, a hand grabbed my wrist and—

. . .

"Xander? *Xander?*"

Sean's voice yanked me out of my nightmare, and as I gripped the duvet and jackknifed up in bed, my eyes darted around a room filled with shadows. It was late, much later than when I'd first gotten into bed, and when Sean sat down on the mattress beside me, I slowly began to make out his silhouette.

Somewhere between now and when I'd fallen asleep, Sean had removed his shirt, and as my mind registered that alarming piece of information, he reached for my face.

"It's okay. You're okay," he said, his voice a velvety baritone that did nothing to ease my already thumping heart.

My eyes flicked around the room again, but when Sean brushed his thumb across my cheek, my attention came back to him.

"Hey there." The twinkling lights from the surrounding buildings caught on his face, and the concern swirling in those dark blue eyes made me tremble. "How you doing?"

I had no idea. The only thing I knew with one hundred percent certainty was how close, and how very naked, Sean seemed to be right now.

"That must've been some dream."

I blinked and knew that if I didn't say something soon he would likely think I was losing it. "More like a nightmare."

"Wanna talk about it?"

"No."

He rubbed his thumb gently over the back of my hand, and I couldn't believe how such a simple gesture was so comforting. There was no awkwardness like at the beginning of all of this. Instead, it felt natural. It felt...right.

"I'm not sure I've said this yet," I said, and licked at my lower lip. "But thank you for being here."

His lips quirked. "In your bedroom?"

"Uh, I meant my house, but I guess right now my bedroom too."

Sean winked at me, and my heart tripped over itself. *Jesus*, when did he develop the ability to make it do that?

"Bet you never thought you'd say that, huh?"

I never thought a lot of things. Like how good his hand would feel holding mine, or how sexy he would look sitting on my bed. But instead of saying any of that, I resorted to our usual behavior and shoved him in the arm.

Sean laughed, seemingly unaffected by my touch.

"I'm serious," he said. "You need me, and for that reason alone, I wouldn't want to be anywhere else."

I nodded, and it wasn't until Sean placed a hand over mine that I realized I'd been trailing my fingers up and down his bicep.

"Sorry," I muttered, and went to pull my hand free. But Sean's fingers tightened, keeping mine in place.

"Don't be. I like it."

"Sean..."

"Xander."

Damn. My name on his tongue sounded better than anything I'd heard in weeks. So damn good that I forgot what I'd been going to say.

"Why don't you move over?" he suggested, and when I

just stared at him like he was speaking another language, he added, "Lie back down and close your eyes. Maybe you'll get some more sleep if I'm here beside you."

Doubtful. Highly, *highly* doubtful. But not having any better ideas, I did what he said. I shifted across my mattress, the sheets on the empty side of the bed cool as they slid over my warm skin, and when Sean pulled back the covers, my head snapped in his direction.

"What are you doing?"

Sean looked down at the bed, and then back to me. "I'm getting under the covers."

"Um…"

A sly grin curved Sean's lips, but instead of wanting to slap him for it, I had a sudden urge to kiss him instead.

"Don't tell me you're shy about having a man in your bed. I have a list that says otherwise." I narrowed my eyes as Sean stood and climbed into the spot I'd just vacated. "Hmm, you warmed it up for me."

Okay, if my body could remember that it was *Sean* getting into bed beside me sometime soon, that would be really helpful.

"You know, the first night I was here and you showed me this room, I imagined how these sheets would feel against me."

Was he kidding right now?

"They looked so expensive and silky."

They were both those things. But to hear Sean talking about it as he lay down and placed his head where mine had just been... My confused body was threatening to embarrass me.

"And man, I was right. They feel fucking amazing. Xander? Did you fall asleep over there?"

"No. Not asleep."

I heard the sheets rustle, and then the mattress dipped down, and as I turned my head on the pillow I could make out the strong lines of Sean's profile.

"So, you wanna talk about it now?"

Talk about...

"That must've been some nightmare."

Oh, right.

"You were breathing really hard, like you were running a marathon. Doesn't take a genius to figure out who you were running from."

I grimaced, but tried to play it off. "Maybe I was running from you. I have been stuck with you for a good two weeks now."

"Best two weeks of your life, no?"

Even though I couldn't see him clearly, I could make out his smile, and after the horrible couple of days I'd just had, it felt nice to want to return it. "It's been...enlightening."

"*Enlightening?* Care to expand on that?"

As I stared across at him in the darkness of my room, I found myself wanting to. Even though every iota of common sense told me to keep my mouth shut. "Well, you're not as... gruff as you want everyone to believe."

"Gruff?"

I tucked a hand under my cheek. "Yes. You act like you're this asshole who doesn't care—"

"Gee, I'm so fucking glad I asked you to expand on this."

I chuckled and couldn't believe how comfortable I felt, lying there in my bed laughing with Sean. *Sean...*

"I'm serious. You act all tough and mean, but I think you do that to keep people at a distance."

"And why would I do that?"

I thought about that for a second—the terrible loss the Bailey brothers had gone through when their parents had passed, and the betrayal of finding out that it had been their father's fault.

"I think you do it because then there's no chance of being hurt or disappointed by those you care about."

Silence fell between us, and I wondered if I'd pushed too far. Then Sean whispered into the night, "You know, I think you might be right."

32

SEAN

SOMETHING WAS HAPPENING to me.

As I lay there in the dark, surrounded by silk sheets and shadows, I had the incredible urge to reach out and touch the man whose bed I had invited myself into only minutes ago.

Yeah, invited myself into. What's that about, Sean?

Xander was only inches from me now, stretched out on his side, and even though the night was concealing his features, I found that I could picture every single one of them as though there was a spotlight on him.

"Sean?"

I felt as though my body were being drawn to him. I felt compelled to move closer, to reach out and touch the one I was sharing this moment with, and I had no idea why.

I was never like this. Never this...vulnerable. I'd always made it a point to keep my guard up. But as I lay there opposite Xander, who was struggling to get through each day at a time, I found myself opening up to him in ways I never imagined possible.

"You're right," I said, thinking about the days, weeks, and months after the car accident that had claimed my parents' lives. "After Mom and Dad died, I shut down. I pushed people away, my family especially. It seemed, I don't know, easier than having to share in their grief. Easier than trying to pretend to be sad when all I was feeling was…"

"It's okay," Xander said, so quietly I barely heard him. "You can say it."

"Intense fucking rage." As the words tumbled off my tongue, the relief I felt was shocking. "I felt murderous. But at the same time weak, and completely and utterly useless. If my father hadn't been killed that night, I swear I would've tracked him down and done the job myself."

Shame flooded me at the very real emotions behind my words. But when Xander reached out and took my hand in his, the lonely space I'd occupied for the last five and a half years felt a little less…lonely.

"Have you ever talked to anyone about this?"

"Like who? Bailey?" Just thinking about that made my gut twist with guilt. How did you admit that instead of grieving the father who raised you, all you felt when he passed was anger? So much goddamn anger. "I don't think so."

"Why not? Do you think he'd somehow think less of you?"

Yeah, I fucking did, and even if he didn't, I thought less of myself. What kind of son was I that I couldn't get past how he died to grieve over the fact that he did?

The covers shifted, and Xander moved closer to me—so close that the glow from the building lights now illuminated his features, and damn, how had I missed what a truly attractive man he was. And more to the point, why was I noticing now?

"Bailey would never judge you for feeling that way."

"Sure he wouldn't."

Xander's fingers tightened around mine, and he jerked me forward as though wanting to shake some sense into me.

"He wouldn't. Just like I'm not judging you for it. Feeling emotions like weakness, anger, and helplessness? They don't make you less in any way, Sean—they're what makes you human."

I swallowed around the lump in my throat, and as I stared into Xander's eyes, my heart began to race, and again I felt it—something was happening to me.

"Sean?"

The sound of my name in that familiar voice sent me into some kind of trance, and I found my mind drifting to things I'd never thought of before. Like how Xander's lips might feel if I were to kiss him right now.

"I'm sorry," he said when I remained mute. "I didn't mean to bring up such a painful memory. I just know how tough this was for Bailey, and I hate to think of you keeping this all to yourself. Then and now."

"Not now," I heard myself say, as I brought his hand up to my chest. "I just shared it with you."

Xander flattened his palm over my heart, and the feel of his hand against my bare skin did nothing to calm the wild beating.

"Sean..." There was no mistaking the breathy catch to his voice.

Xander was aroused, and to my complete shock, so was I.

"What are we doing here?"

I had no fucking clue. One minute I'd been trying to comfort him, and the next I was thinking about how it might feel to kiss him.

Thump. Thump. Thump. There was that heavy pounding again. My heart beating so loud that I was surprised he couldn't hear it. I could smell whatever soap and shampoo he'd used in the shower, and as the scent wrapped around me, I stopped thinking of him as my brother's best friend, and instead started thinking about how right it felt to be here with him in his bed.

Fuck.

Xander raised his face to mine, and when our eyes locked I saw the same desire I'd heard in his voice just seconds ago. *Jesus*, that look was as terrifying as it was hot, because I wasn't sure what to do next.

"Sean, whatever it is you think you're feeling right now, it's not real—"

"I don't know about that," I said, and before I knew what

I was doing, I was trailing my fingers along his jaw. "It feels pretty fucking real to me."

Xander trembled and reached for my hand, halting it. "It's not. It's just the circumstance, that's all. The night, the close confines—"

"The man? Come on, Xander. You think I would feel this way with just anyone? Let alone a *guy*? I don't think it's a particular set of circumstances that has me rock hard right now—I think it's you, and I think it's me. Tell me you aren't wondering what it would feel like to kiss me. Go on, tell me."

Xander swallowed, but said nothing.

"You can't, can you?"

"It's doesn't matter. It's totally different for me than it is for you."

"How?"

"Because I'm gay, and I know better than to take advantage of whatever it is you think you're feeling."

"What I *think* I'm feeling?" I reached for his chin and angled his face so my mouth was hovering over his. "So I don't really want to kiss you, is that what you're trying to tell me?"

"I didn't say that. I just want to make sure that you—"

Before he could finish, my mouth was on his. Xander froze and shoved me back, and for a split second I wondered if I'd read this completely wrong—then it happened.

Xander lunged forward, crashed his mouth down on top of mine, and took my lips in a kiss that I hadn't realized I craved until now.

Hard. Rough. And full of pent-up desire. Xander's lips were everything I'd never known I was missing, and when his tongue slid along my lower one seeking permission for entrance, I opened to him in a fucking heartbeat.

Xander moaned low in his throat as his tongue slipped past that first barrier, and when he speared his fingers into my hair and I arched back into his touch, our bodies came into direct—and very intimate—contact.

"Shit," he said against my lips, and then pulled his mouth free. "This is crazy."

And really fucking hot. Never in a million years could I have imagined ending up in bed with Xander, and just as I was about to tell him that, he brought his hands down to my chest and gave a gentle shove.

Hang on a second, what is he—

"Sean, we need to stop."

It took a hot second for that to compute, but when it did, the first thing that entered my mind was that I had done something wrong, or worse, Xander just wasn't into it.

"Did I do something you didn't like?"

"What?" Xander shook his head. "No. No. But this...this complicates things, Sean. It's not just a kiss, especially not with you."

"Why the fuck not?"

Xander sighed and rubbed his face. "For so many reasons. But off the top of my head, you've never been with a man before. And what about Bailey? There's so much to think about if we..."

"If we what?" I said, not willing, for some reason, to let go of the idea of never being able to do this with him again.

"If we take this any further. Emotions are running high right now, and maybe we need to just stop and, I don't know, sleep on it."

He was right. I knew he was. But the second I rolled away from him, my body tensed, rebelling against the move. It didn't want to leave—the bed or the man—and wasn't that a fucking head-trip?

"Sean?"

I stopped on the second step of the bed's platform and looked back at where Xander sat in the shadows.

"Yeah?"

"I'm sorry."

I had no idea what he was apologizing for, considering I planned to get back to this conversation in the morning, but before I could say that, he scooted down in bed, and I took that to mean that the conversation was done.

I made my way to the settee and took up a position where I could keep an eye on him, and I wondered if Xander was reliving what had just happened the way I was. Because shit, that had been one of the hottest kisses I'd ever had.

I brought my fingers to my lips, remembering the delicious pressure of Xander's as he'd practically devoured me, and while I knew he thought I was confused about what I was feeling, one thing I wasn't confused about was how fucking hard I was.

Xander... I was sitting here with a hard-on for Xander. Confusing wasn't the right word. Mind-blowing might be closer. That I'd somehow walked through life and never really looked at one of the people who was in it.

But I was looking now, and as I grabbed one of the couch pillows and settled in for the night, my eyes locked on the man I'd known for as long as I could remember, and I felt as though I were seeing him for the very first time—and damn if I didn't like the view.

33

XANDER

I WOKE LATE, and I woke alone. A weird sensation when just the night before this bed had been full of emotions so explosive they had nearly ignited the sheets.

I wasn't surprised Sean had left, though. If anything, I'd been shocked he wanted to stay after the way things had ended. But it seemed he'd been eager for some space of his own the second the night had passed.

I closed my eyes for a minute and allowed myself to remember the moment when Sean had changed from an all-round nuisance to the man who'd reawakened my body with just one kiss—and what a kiss it had been. Sean kissed like he did everything else, arrogantly, and while it might've been the first time he'd ever kissed a man, by the end of it, he'd been all in.

I let out a sigh and opened my eyes. This morning was going to be tense for reasons that had nothing to do with a hot kiss, and everything to do with me putting a halt to things. But one thing my parents had drilled into me from a young age was that there were always consequences to my actions. In the case of Sean and me, there would be many.

That didn't mean I hadn't wanted it, though. Hadn't wanted *him*. And even after he'd taken up his original spot in my sitting area, I hadn't been able to take my eyes off him —and vice versa.

It had been one of the longest, most frustrating nights of my life, and what had started out as curiosity when it came to Sean Bailey had now turned into a deep, insistent longing that I had no idea how to crush.

Shoving aside the sheet, I spotted a note on my bedside table with *Mornin', Anchorman* scrawled across the top. Picking it up, I read over the words, and despite the fact Sean had left before I'd even opened my eyes, I found a smile crossing my face.

I NEEDED *to make some calls. Come find me when you wake.*
    The place has already been cleared.
    - Sean
    P.S. I woke up super hungry this morning. Hope you did too...

IT WAS difficult to tell if this note was meant to be the double entendre I read it as. But knowing Sean, and the way any joke of a sexual nature—especially a gay one—flew over his head, my thoughts were that he probably had just woken up...hungry.

That didn't help the throb that had again started between my legs, however, and, deciding I needed to get dressed and get out of this room, where the memories of that kiss were swirling in my head, I made my way to the bathroom for a quick shower before facing the day.

A quick *cold* shower.

THE SOUND OF a sizzling pan greeted me when I stepped out of my bedroom around fifteen minutes later, and the tantalizing smell of bacon not long after that.

I made my way down the hall, and when I rounded the corner into my kitchen to see Sean standing at the oven in a pair of cargo shorts and one of those tight t-shirts he favored, my conscience, which had been so loud the night before, suddenly became very hard to hear.

How had I missed what a phenomenal body he had all these years? Those crumpled work suits had been hiding a seriously powerful physique. One I wanted to feel against me, doing things I never imagined wanting with Sean.

Pushing that thought aside, I reminded myself just how dangerous it was to think of my best friend's brother this way. No matter how damn attractive he was.

"Good morning," I said.

Sean glanced in my direction, and as his eyes trailed down over my white linen shirt and plum-colored Bermuda shorts, it became apparent that the bacon wasn't the only thing now hot in the kitchen.

"Mornin'."

One word—that was apparently all it took for my brain to forget how to function and my cock to eagerly take its place. But I wasn't going to give in. Consequences were a real thing.

I swallowed and tried to bank the urge to kiss him again, just to see if it would be as intense and addictive as last night.

Instead, I looked to the pan and nodded. "Smells good."

"Yeah?" Sean grinned. "Wasn't sure you were a big breakfast kind of guy. I've only ever seen you inhale coffee and eat cereal."

Happy to see he wasn't about to make things awkward, I moved around him and headed to the fridge, where I grabbed the juice from the top shelf.

"That's the standard for sure. But obviously you found my stash of bacon, sooo..."

"Clearly we're a match made in heaven."

I froze where I stood by the fridge, and then Sean looked my way and laughed.

"You should see your face right now."

I could imagine. But hearing him talk about us in such a casually intimate way did things to my... Well, my entire body. Not entirely unpleasant things, either.

"Relax, Xander. It's not like I suddenly think we're soul mates." As Sean looked back to the bacon, he chuckled.

"Even if you do kiss like you should be giving a master class on it."

Okay. I hadn't been sure if last night was a result of specific circumstances or a mutual attraction. But this time when Sean glanced my way, there were no shadows to conceal the arousal swirling in his eyes.

I slowly shut the fridge door and placed the juice on the counter. "A master class, huh? That's a pretty high compliment."

Sean's eyes fell to my mouth, and damn if I could remember the reasons why this—whatever *this* was—was a bad idea.

"Well, it was a pretty hot fucking kiss."

I had to hand it to him. Sean was as blunt as one could be, and for the first time since I'd known him, I couldn't have been happier for it. Nor could I keep the grin off my lips.

"What?" Sean said, making my smile grow even wider.

"Nothing. I was just wondering if you ever imagined saying those words to me."

"Well, no. But then again, I never imagined watching you sleep would make me hard as a fucking rock, but..."

I knew I should stop this conversation. Head it off at the pass while I still could. But instead of doing that, instead of listening to my brain and heeding its advice, I reached over to the stove and turned off the burner.

Sean glanced down at where my fingers rested on the knob in front of him. When he let go of the pan and placed the tongs down on the counter, I touched my fingers to the hem of his shirt and said, "But what?"

34

SEAN

FUCK. THIS WAS about to get all kinds of complicated, judging by the stiff dick in my pants and pounding of my heart.

When Xander had put an end to things last night, I hadn't really known what to expect this morning. I knew he'd done it in part because he thought I didn't know what I was feeling. But as the memories of that kiss flashed behind my eyes, the blinding arousal that had overtaken me made it impossible to deny the truth—and the truth was that Xander turned me on.

It was new, a little strange, and a whole lot overwhelming. But when he flattened his palm against my abdomen and shoved me away from the stove, there was no way I was about to stop him. I'd wanted this from the second I'd heard his bedroom door open this morning, and when my ass came up against the kitchen island, I took a nice, long look at him.

Dressed for the blistering heat forecasted for today,

Xander was in a cool white shirt and a pair of shorts that molded so well to his body that I had no problem making out his erection. I was aware that should probably freak me the fuck out, but it didn't. Not with the way he was looking at me.

"It seems," I said, finally getting back to Xander's original question, "everything about you makes me hard these days."

Xander licked his bottom lip, and I nodded.

"Yeah, especially that. Don't ask me when it changed or why I can't stop thinking about anything other than your mouth. But fuck me, it's the truth."

Xander angled his head so he was looking up at me, and I wondered how I'd gone through life not realizing just how perfect his face was.

"Are you sure?"

"Sure that I want to kiss you again?"

Xander looked me directly in the eye. "If that's all there is to it, then yes—"

"It's not." The words were out of my mouth before I could think them through. But ever since he'd stepped into the kitchen, I'd been craving a reconnection that had nothing to do with a kiss and everything to do with being as close to him as I could physically get. "I mean, the kissing is part of it. I feel like I'd walk through a fire to kiss you again. But it's more than that, and I think you know it. Otherwise you wouldn't be worried about this getting so...complicated."

"Right." His fingers crept under my shirt, and when they touched my skin and I sucked in a breath, Xander asked, "And this? Are you sure you want *me* touching you like this?"

There was more to that question than what he'd just asked. Xander wanted to know if I was okay with a *man* touching me. It'd been one of the main reasons he'd put a stop to this last night, and I couldn't blame him.

Two weeks ago I never could've imagined having this conversation. But something had changed in that time. Being this close to Xander felt like second nature, allowing a transition from friend to much more to be easier than I had ever expected.

But how was he supposed to know that unless I told him? Unless I showed him exactly what I was feeling.

I shoved away from the counter and turned us until he was up against it. Then I took his chin again and lowered my head until my lips were ghosting over his. "Why don't you touch me again, and I'll let you know."

Xander's eyes blazed as he drew his fingers across the tight skin of my stomach.

"Oh yeah, I definitely want you to keep doing that."

Xander's lips curved, and the smile was so sensual I had to brace my hands on the counter behind him to keep my legs from giving out under me.

"You do, do you?"

"Fuck yes."

He leaned forward a fraction and placed his lips against my jaw. "And what about this? Do you like this?" He slid his hands up my torso, my shirt moving up with them, as he began to kiss and bite his way along my jaw line.

I pressed my fingers into the granite countertop as he continued to tease and torment me, and fuck, never had I been so close to falling at someone's feet. He moved in to kiss behind my ear, and when his hands slid around to my back and down to my ass, I had to grind my teeth together to control myself.

"Sean," he said, then Xander raised his head, flames flickering in his eyes. As our lower bodies bumped up against each other, I ground myself on him, and the hard pressure against my aching shaft was the best thing I'd felt in my life.

"Convinced I want this yet?"

Xander wrapped his arms around my neck and rocked into me. "Nearly."

I growled against his lips and reached for his hips, still wanting him closer. When he raised a leg to wrap it around one of my thighs, an idea struck. I smoothed my hands down to the back of his legs so I could get a good grip, and then I lifted him up onto his counter.

When his ass hit the granite, Xander spread his legs wide, and I gripped his waist to tug him as close to the edge of the counter as possible.

Xander smoothed his hands down over my chest and slowly shook his head. "Damn, I really wish you didn't feel this good."

"It's a bad thing?"

"No. It's a frustrating thing. But I'm done pretending, Sean. I'm done trying to hide how I feel around you. I want you. I've wanted you for days now. But I don't want to rush you into anything."

"You're not."

He chuckled and then nipped at my lower lip, and I couldn't stop my groan. "Maybe not right now, but if we keep going, I will."

His raspy tone made my knees feel weak, not to mention all that he was implying, and just as I was about to ask him for specifics, the lights in the kitchen flickered.

Xander frowned and looked up at the three that hung over the counter. "It must be the heat. They said it would be bad today—"

"I don't care about that." And I really didn't. I wanted to know where he would push me if we kept on with the kissing.

"No?"

"No."

Xander laughed, and the sound did crazy things to my already tripping heart.

"You might change your mind if you get stuck in the elevator."

"Not if I get stuck with you."

As he gave me a thorough once-over, my cock stood up tall and paid really close attention. Oh yeah, there was no doubt about who *it* wanted to be stuck with.

"Are you flirting with me?"

Unbelievable as it was, my cheeks heated at Xander's question. I went to step away so he wouldn't see he was right, but he wound his legs around the backs of my thighs and grabbed onto my hands.

"Wait, are you blushing?"

There was no way I was admitting to that. "No."

"Yes, you are."

"I'm—"

"Blushing."

When I glared at him, Xander arched a brow, and the move was so uppity, so *him*, that I found myself reaching out and tracing my finger over it just because I could.

"Why are you embarrassed?"

"I don't know, it's just..." I let out a sigh. "I don't do this kind of thing."

"What, flirting? Hmm." Xander pulled me back in close to him. "Well, I liked it. The flirting and the blushing."

I gave him a pointed look, and Xander grinned and slid down off the counter. He placed a hand on my chest and said, "I also kind of like that grumpy Detective *Dick* isn't all that grumpy around me."

"I don't know about that. You keep up with this kissing and stopping bullshit and I might get grumpy real quick."

Xander slipped out from between me and the counter and snagged a piece of bacon, then he looked down to my still-erect cock.

"I don't think so. But if that happens, a simple kiss should cure the problem. As far as I can tell, they make you much more agreeable."

"Uh-huh, except there was nothing simple about that kiss."

"You're right," he said, and then stepped out into the hall. "That's why I'm going to go and do some work. But I'm really glad we had this little...talk."

As he went to walk off, I quickly moved out in the hallway and shouted, "That's it?"

Xander looked back at me and grinned. "Definitely not. But it was a really good start."

He then bit into his bacon and disappeared down the hall, and the second he was gone, everything became crystal clear.

I wanted Alexander Thorne, and by some miracle of fate, he wanted me right back.

35

XANDER

"WANT TO GET out of here for a bit?"

I looked up to see Sean in the entryway of the seating area I'd run away to earlier. I wondered how long he'd been waiting to come and ask me that.

I loved this space. It was at the east end of the building, and in the winter it benefited from all the warmth of the morning sun. This morning, however, I had the shades drawn. I was curled up in a plush oversized chair with my feet propped up on the matching ottoman, and as Sean walked into the room, I saved the document I was working on and looked up from my laptop.

"Get out of here? There's a heatwave going on today. Did you miss the memo?"

"No, but I thought you might want to take a walk or something before it gets too hot. You know, get some fresh air."

My lips twitched. Not because it was a bad suggestion,

but because the last thing I could ever imagine Sean wanting was to go for a walk to get some "fresh air."

"Feeling a little cooped up?" I asked as I closed the laptop and slid it onto the table beside me.

"Hard to feel cooped up in this place. But it's a nice day, and I thought you might want to get outside for a bit before you head in tonight."

That was a nice enough answer, but I thought this was more about spending time together than heading outside for a stretch. Sean missed me, and I had to admit, I missed him too.

I smiled at the thought, and as I got to my feet, I noticed he was holding a book.

"You read?"

Sean lifted the novel and then smirked. "No need to sound so shocked. I can do basic math, too."

My mouth fell open, and when Sean chuckled, I shook my head. "I didn't mean it like that."

"No?"

"No. I guess I didn't expect it, that's all." When Sean just stood there staring at me—or judging my, what did he call them? Upper-class ways—I snatched the book from his hand.

When I flipped it over and caught sight of *The Stand*, I raised a brow. "Stephen King, huh?"

"Yep. It's one of my favorites. I love the epic battle of good versus evil in a post-apocalyptic setting, and the plethora of well-developed characters is just mind-blowing. I've read it several times now. Both versions."

Completely and utterly gob-smacked, I stood there for a moment trying to reconcile this Sean with the one I'd grown up with. But I was starting to realize that those two people were very different. Or maybe they'd just never been in my presence at the same time before now.

"Xander?"

"Sorry. I'm..." I paused and tapped my fingers on the front cover of the book. "I'm just trying to wrap my head around the fact that you used the word *plethora* in a sentence."

"Impressed?"

I was. I was also ashamed that I'd had such a narrow-minded view of him. What other secrets was Sean hiding? "Maybe a little."

"Bullshit." Sean grabbed the book out of my hand and tossed it on the couch. "You're totally fucking impressed. Admit it."

His smug smile was hard to refuse, but I bit down on the inside of my cheek and tried for my most serious expression. "I'm innocent, detective. I swear."

Sean's eyes darkened and my blood began to hum. Then he stepped in close to me and reached for my hand. When his fingers interlaced with mine, my breath got caught in my throat.

"Come for a walk with me."

How could I refuse? I glanced at the clock over on the wall; it was just going on ten. "Okay. But we can't be gone long. I have to get back to head in—"

"By eleven. I know your schedule, anchorman. I'll get you where you need to go on time."

My stomach flipped at this new nickname Sean had been using around me the past couple of days, and I'd be lying if I said I didn't like it.

I did...a lot.

"Then let's go. There's this little place on the corner that I always—"

"No," Sean interrupted, which made me automatically bristle.

"No?"

"No. When are you going to understand that you can't go to the places you always go, Xander? Which reminds me, we need to have a talk about who can, and cannot, come here while this is all going on."

I tried not to take the dressing down to heart, but the condescending tone after such a personal moment made my hackles rise. "Oh? And who might that be?"

Sean eyed me for a beat, my frosty response clearly making him second-guess his approach. But then he seemed to decide: in for a penny, in for a pound.

"No fucking one, that's who. It's just you and me until this is all over."

Right. Pulling my hand free, I narrowed my eyes and said, "I think I've changed my mind. I don't want to go for that walk after all."

As I went to step around him, Sean reached out and grabbed my wrist, hauling me back to face him.

"Why are you so mad?"

"Why are you such a...*dick?*"

Sean's jaw twitched. "I'm just trying to keep you safe. And letting people into your house right now is—"

"Stupid, *I* know. Don't you think I'm aware of what an idiot I was yesterday? Trust me, I got that loud and clear. But it's hard to readjust your habits and your life with a snap of your fingers."

I let out a sigh. "I'm trying, Sean. I really am. But sometimes I forget things like letting my front desk guy bring up a flower delivery, or going to the corner park near my building..."

"That's why I'm here." Sean gently tugged me back to him and grazed his thumb over the back of my hand. "If you're not sure of something, wait for my cue."

My heart thumped at his gentle tone and sincerity. "And what's this cue?"

Sean looked down at our hands and shrugged. "I don't know. Sorry I'm a jackass?"

I chuckled. "That works."

"I just want you safe. I *need* you safe, Xander."

A shiver raced up my spine as we stood there toe to toe, and I knew if we didn't get out of there, things were going to go from zero to sixty in a heartbeat. He was too close, he smelled too good, and the look in his eyes spoke of things I knew he wasn't ready for just yet—no matter how convincing he might be otherwise.

"I'm sorry I worried you yesterday." I gently pulled my hand free. "I promise to think first and act later."

As I took a step back, Sean smirked. "Is that what you're doing now?"

"What do you mean?"

"Are you *thinking* before you act?" Sean moved toward me, and I took several steps back. "Or maybe you're running so you *don't* act."

"I'm not running anywhere. But if we don't leave now, this little walk of yours isn't going to happen."

It was a good enough answer, but I could tell by Sean's smug look that he didn't buy it for a second. That was too bad, however—it was the only answer he was going to get, because if I stayed here any longer, I couldn't be held responsible for what I did next.

36

SEAN

"HEY, MAC, IT'S Sean. Is Nichols there?"

Around fifteen minutes later, I found myself waiting outside a small boutique bakery three blocks west of Xander's building, with the phone glued to my ear and my eyes scanning the street.

Xander's morning jogs usually took him up east, where there was a small park and a coffee vendor he frequented. But after discovering this little gem and seeing the delicious goodies inside, I had a feeling he would be putting in a few extra miles when he was back to his usual routine, just to make sure he passed by this place on the way back.

"Sean?" Nichols barked through the phone, and I focused my attention back on the reason I was calling.

Nichols was a buddy of mine back at the precinct, and had been helping me out by digging a little deeper on the car's license plate from the attempted hit-and-run. He'd also agreed to attend tomorrow's award ceremony, and for that, I'd owe him.

"Yeah, it's me. Listen, I was wondering if you could take a look at something for me today. This fucker showed up again yesterday."

"You've got to be kidding me. That's twice in one week."

"Three times, actually. Seems I'm pissing him off."

"Well, we all have our strengths. Pissing people off is definitely one of yours. Of course I'll help. Just know I'm writing all this shit down for an IOU later."

I didn't doubt it for a second. "Florist shop. The Crimson Petal. Some flowers were delivered yesterday from there, but when I called the number on it, they said they closed at noon. I mean, who closes at noon on a Thursday? I don't know. But could you go over there and check it out for me? I'd do it myself, but—"

"You've got to keep your eye on your guy, I know."

My stomach did a somersault, and I quickly thought back over my words to see if I'd said something to make Nichols think Xander was more to me than just a client.

I mean, he was, but—*my guy?* He wasn't mine... *Fuck. Stop reading into it.* "That is the job."

"A lucrative one too, huh? Everyone's buzzing about you taking care of the golden boy of the news world."

They were? Great, that was just what I needed. "Well, tell everyone to mind their own fucking business. Someone's threatening his life. How would they feel if they were in his position and people were busy gossiping about them instead of giving a shit?"

"Jesus, Sean. Calm down. All I meant was that they wished *they* were the ones trailing him. You're gonna have a nice retirement egg after this. They're jealous."

Fuck that. I wasn't doing this for the money, and the idea that anyone would think that I was—that *Xander* might think that—made me want to punch something.

"Can you check out the florist or not?"

"Yeah, text me the address and what you want to know. I'll call you later today with what I find out."

I muttered a quick goodbye and then turned to look in the window of the bakery, where Xander was now perusing the baked goods behind the glass display.

There were three other people inside the place with him: a woman stocked shelves at one end, while a young man behind the counter refilled the little cake boxes on the back shelf, and sitting at one of the small tables and chairs was the only other customer, a man who looked to be closing in on his seventies.

The sun blistered the back of my neck as I kept my eyes on Xander, and when he smiled at something the young man said, there was a tightening in my chest that had nothing to do with fear, and everything to do with these new feelings that were tap-dancing around inside me.

This was getting real. The feelings, the emotions, the desire I had to be near Xander at all times now—it extended beyond wanting to keep him safe. If I were honest with myself, it'd stopped being about that days ago. Now it was about wanting to be near him, period, and wasn't *that* eye-opening?

As a spark of recognition lit the young man's face, he grinned and began talking to Xander as though he'd known him his whole life. Xander returned the easy conversation—of course he did—and when he flashed his famous smile, I found myself getting irritated that I wasn't the one making him smile.

And what the hell was that about? Xander didn't belong to me, not in any way at all. But it didn't seem to matter. Not to my brain, and certainly not to my stomach, which was churning with a new kind of emotion—envy. I wanted to be the one making him forget about the last two shitty weeks, not be the sole reminder of it.

As Xander handed over his card and paid for his pastry, I turned away to do another quick sweep of the surrounding road and walkways, and when I was satisfied nothing looked suspicious, I looked back inside to see Xander heading for the doors.

I jogged over to pull one of them open for him, and when his eyes landed on me, a smile slowly spread across his lips. Right there, in the blink of an eye, the irritation I'd felt seconds earlier vanished. Because while Xander might've been chatting it up with that guy as though he was the most entertaining person he'd spoken to in weeks, this smile was personal and intimate, and I wouldn't have traded it for the world.

"Thank you."

"Sure thing." I gestured to the paper bag he held. "What'd you get?"

Xander swung the sack between us and said, "Guess."

As we walked up the sidewalk, I looked at him out of the corner of my eye. "Hmm, well, if they had turnovers, I think you got one of those. Maybe an apple one?"

Xander stopped in his tracks and turned to look at me with his mouth hanging open. "How on earth did you know that?"

I took the bag from him and peered inside, and yep, there was the apple turnover. "You get them all the time. Whenever you bring pastries on Saturdays you get a caramel walnut roll for Bay, double chunk chip cookies for Kieran, and"—I stuck my hand inside the bag—"a lemon bar for me."

When I flashed a grin at Xander, he chuckled and shook his head. "You're observant."

I bit down into the tangy lemon curd and chewed, then I did something I'd never done in my life: I winked at him. "It's kind of my job."

Xander licked at his bottom lip, drawing my eyes like a fucking magnet, and when he reached out to run his thumb across the corner of my mouth, my dick jerked.

"You had powdered sugar on your face," he said, and then licked his thumb clean.

Fuckin' hell. I wanted to kiss him so badly that it was a miracle I didn't drag him down to the sidewalk. Instead, I reached for his hand, and when he automatically took it, I marveled at how natural it now felt.

"Ready to head back?"

Xander nodded, and we began to make our way back to his building. We were one block over when he said, "This was a great idea. Thanks for getting me out of the house."

"I have them occasionally."

"You have them all the time." Xander paused and looked down to our hands. "Like this whole undercover thing. You knew it would work, when I didn't think it would."

That wasn't exactly true, but... "I just figured it would be the easiest way."

"Easiest?" Xander laughed. "I'm not sure any of my past boyfriends would agree with that."

"Then they're fucking idiots." *Except Bay,* I quickly amended in my head.

"I swear, when I talk to you lately, I feel like I'm getting to know someone I've never met before. How is that possible when I've known you most of my life?"

I took the final bite of my lemon bar and sucked the residual sugar from my thumb. "Maybe it wasn't time yet."

"Time for what?"

"To notice each other."

Xander angled his head to the side, studying me closely. "And is that what we're doing now? Noticing each other?"

I couldn't stop myself. I reached out and brushed my fingers across the thick hair that had swept down across his forehead. "Oh yeah. I'm noticing all kinds of things about you, Mr. Anchorman."

Like his heavy-lidded expression. He liked me touching him like this.

"Is this payback?"

"Payback?"

"Yes. For me kissing and stopping?"

I let out a low chuckle and let my hand fall back down to my side. "Maybe. Is it working?"

Xander's gaze fell to my lips, and I had my answer even before he said it.

"Yes, I think it is."

When we reached the front entrance of his building, I pulled open one of the doors for him and, still caught up in the man beside me, didn't realize until the last second that one of the cleaners had been wiping down the glass.

I quickly apologized, but he brushed it off with a wave of his hand, and we headed to Xander's private elevator.

As we stood there, shoulder to shoulder, he flashed me that hot smirk I was starting to recognize as flirting. Then he said something that proved that he was much better at this game of cat and mouse than I was.

"So, maybe tonight when we get home, you can tell me some of the things you've noticed about me."

Game. Set. Match.

And though Xander had just won fair and square, I in no way felt like a loser.

"HAVE YOU EVER seen a live broadcast before?"

I turned to see Ryan walking over to the check-in desk where I stood and shook my head.

I was there tonight under the guise of bringing Xander dinner, but I wasn't about to miss out on an opportunity to get my eyes on the man I couldn't stop thinking about. I happily followed Ryan through to Control Room A and took the headset he held out to me.

"Just take a seat over here, and when everything gets going you'll be able to hear."

"Awesome. Thanks."

"No problem. I gotta run."

Before I could say anything else, Ryan disappeared out of the room, and I turned back to face the wall of monitors.

One showed the local news that came on before Xander's nightly broadcast. Another had the stock market graphs and values ticking along the bottom of the screen. Then there was the international sister station of ENN, and on the massive monitor in the middle of all of that chaos was a still of Xander's logo, *Global News with Alexander Thorne,* with a countdown clock above it that currently had five minutes remaining.

Men and women were bustling around the room punching buttons on elaborate control panels and barking out orders to one another. The glass doors behind me pushed open and Jim—Xander's EP—walked through, grabbed a headset, and shoved it onto his head.

"We all ready to go in here?" he asked.

"Yep, ready to roll."

"Okay." Jim clipped a battery pack—or something like it —onto his belt, then nodded to the woman sitting directly in front of a massive control panel. With several flicks of the switches on the board, the logo vanished and Xander appeared sitting behind his desk, where he was reading over something in front of him. "Everything looking good, boss?"

Xander looked up, staring directly into the camera focused on him. He'd changed from his shorts and shirt into a pristine black suit and snowy-white button-down and teal tie, and wow, the things it did to his hair and eyes were... Well, they were fucking stunning.

As I shifted in my seat, reminding my body I was out in public and it needed to behave itself, Xander smoothed a hand down the front of his tie and pulled his chair in further under the desk.

"Everything's good. Were we able to update the graphics for the opening story? I heard the number of people reported without electricity changed a couple of minutes ago."

"We're working on it now," someone in the far left of the control room called out, and Jim relayed the info back to Xander.

"Very good. I expect the number will change again midway through the broadcast, so can we make sure to be on that so we can update everyone by the end of the program?"

"On it already," Jim said.

"Okay, then I'm good."

Jim barked out a few more orders, and then he glanced around the control room. His eyes caught on me and he paused. "Ah. It looks like you've got a live audience tonight, Mr. Thorne. Sean's here."

When Xander frowned, Jim smirked at me.

"Want to wish him luck?"

For a second, I wondered why Jim found it necessary to tell him that I was there. Who cared if I was or not? But then

I remembered Xander's comment about Jim finding us an unlikely match and wondered if this was a test or some shit.

Well, if it was, I was about to pass with flying colors.

Jim walked over and pressed a button on a table mic in front of me. "You just talk in here."

"Got it." I pushed the button, looked up at the screen, and said, "Hey there, anchorman."

Xander smiled, and any thought other than him vanished from my mind.

"You scrub up real good, you know that?"

Xander chuckled, and then looked directly down the camera and said, "I'm glad you finally noticed."

At the not-so-subtle reminder of our discussion this afternoon, I swallowed back a groan. "Have a good show."

"I will now. See you in thirty minutes."

I took my finger off the button and sat back in my seat, and when I looked up at Jim, I noticed his eyes had narrowed a fraction. Guy was acting really fucking odd, and before I could ask him if there was a problem with me being there, he turned and headed back to the center of the room.

"Okay, Xander. You're on in thirty."

The countdown began, and when it hit *three, two, one* and the promo and music for the broadcast began, my phone vibrated in my pocket.

I pulled it out to see it was Nichols calling me back. Just as I got to my feet, Xander appeared on the screen and said, "Good evening, and welcome to Global News this Friday evening. I'm Alexander Thorne..."

Damn it. I really wouldn't have minded watching him for the next half-hour, but I needed to take this call.

I headed out of the control room, brought the phone to my ear, and answered.

"Hello, Sean here."

"Hey, man, how's it going?"

"It's going."

"Yeah, I feel you." Nichols sighed. "These blackouts are getting out of hand tonight."

"No shit. Got to love Chicago in the summer."

"I don't know about that, but the winters are fucking worse, sooo..." Nichols chuckled, and then quickly sobered up. "Sorry, but I'm not calling with anything good. First up, I might as well tell you, we still got nothing on the plate. Could be it was stolen, switched out, or God knows what, but there's no car matching your description with that plate as far as we can tell right now."

Shit. I'd hoped that wasn't what was holding things up, but I'd begun to suspect that was the case. God, sometimes I really hated being right. "What about the florist?"

"Same deal, kinda. No delivery guy matching the description you gave works there. Just two lovely ladies and a middle-aged man who owns the shop. I asked about who placed the order, and they said it was done online."

"Of course it was. So who picked them up? Who delivered them?"

"They said they use independent delivery guys or messengers on busy days."

"And let me guess, that day was busy."

236ELLA FRANK

"You got it."

I cursed and ran a hand through my hair down to the back of my neck. I was hitting one roadblock after another. "Well, thanks for fucking nothing, Nichols."

"Yeah. I know. I told you I wasn't calling with anything good."

"Let me know if anything hits on the license plate. I won't hold my breath."

"Probably a smart idea. I'll see you at the dinner tomorrow night."

"Yeah, see ya there," I said. As I hung up, I looked at Studio A's doors and the bright red light above it with the words ON AIR. I wished I could keep Xander in there.

Safe behind a locked door and camera, where I could keep my eyes on him at all times. Safe from this lunatic who was hunting him down.

37

XANDER

I'D NEVER BEEN more thankful in my life to see that the power was still on in my building. Sean parked his SUV and we headed across the lot to the elevator.

It was a chance riding it up to my floor for sure, but what was the alternative? Trek up twenty-five flights of stairs in this heat? I wouldn't have opted for that on any night of the week. But when I added in the desperate hunger I had to be somewhere alone with Sean, that idea was definitely off the table.

This morning felt as though it had happened years ago, not hours, and the tension that had been building between us was close to fever pitch as the elevator finally hit my floor and the doors slowly slid open.

Sean stepped out first, and when I followed close on his heels, he said, "Don't move. This is just gonna take me a minute."

He disappeared down the hall to the gym and bedroom areas, and I thought it a shame I couldn't just follow and stay in one of them with him. But now more than ever, I understood the importance of making sure things were clear before going further, because if this psycho had been in my house, the last thing I wanted was to meet up with him somewhere in the dark.

A shudder racked my body, but when Sean marched back up the hall, I quickly shoved it aside. I wasn't going to let fear and worry ruin my night. I'd let this creep into too many facets of my life already, but tonight I planned to enjoy myself as though that asshole didn't exist.

"All clear?" I asked as Sean got closer, and I had to slip my hands into my pockets so I didn't do anything stupid, like grab him and shove him up against the nearest wall.

"Those rooms are," he said. "Let me check out the rest of the house real quick."

The serious tone and expression on his face was so damn hot I was having difficulty remembering the reason he was checking things. But I nodded and took great pleasure in watching him stride off down my hall.

Who knew what a fine ass Sean Bailey had? Or that watching him throw around his authoritative side would get me so damn hot?

If someone had told me that at the beginning of all of this, I would've laughed them out of the building. But when Sean re-entered the hall and crooked a finger at me, my cock didn't find anything funny about the action at all. It found it all kinds of sexy.

"Clear?" I asked again, as I entered the kitchen to see Sean by the open doors of the terrace. He'd left the kitchen lights on, a move that was no doubt designed to make me feel more secure.

"All clear." Sean was about to close the doors when I shook my head.

"Leave them open. It's a nice night." I walked over to him and enjoyed the breeze that drifted by.

"Do you want something to eat?" Sean asked. "I could make us something."

I appreciated the offer, but there was only one thing I was hungry for, and it wasn't food.

"Xander?"

This was it. This was where I either ended everything and chalked last night up to crazed emotions, or...

I reached for Sean's hand, and when his fingers slipped between mine, I stepped outside and tugged him along with me.

Sean said nothing as I led him over to the rail, and somewhere in the back of my mind I was aware that it had been the night out here on this terrace that my feelings had begun to cross the line.

That was the night I'd known I was in trouble, and as I stood here now, with a multimillion-dollar view surrounding me, and Sean the only thing I wanted to look at, I knew I'd moved beyond the point where I could fool myself.

I wanted to be with Sean, in any way he'd have me. When he raised our hands so mine was resting flat against his chest, I could feel his heart thumping steadily beneath it.

It was peaceful, calm, one of the most beautiful moments of my life, and it was hard to remember that outside of this bubble, the rest of my life was in complete chaos.

"I heard back from the precinct—"

"No," I interrupted, and pressed a finger against his lips. "Not tonight. Can we just have one night where we don't talk about this? Where I pretend that everything in my life is normal?"

"I hope not, because then you might stop touching me."

"On the contrary: touching you is quickly becoming one of the most normal things in the world to me."

"Xander... Shit." Sean wound an arm around my waist and slowly drew me in, then he lowered his head to rest his forehead to mine. "There's so much about this that I don't understand."

"I know," I said, as his heart thumped a little faster beneath my palm. "And if you don't want to go any further, I—

"No. That's not what I meant."

"It's not?"

"No. I meant that I don't understand how I didn't see you all this time. You were right there, and I..."

"I feel the same way."

"You do?"

"I really do."

Sean smirked. "I mean, then there's the fact that you're a guy." Just when I thought he might let go, his fingers tightened around my waist and he whispered, "But that doesn't seem to matter anymore. I want you anyway."

I groaned and turned my mouth into his, and the second they connected there was no looking back. His lips parted and I entered, and when my tongue got the first taste of his, my knees close to buckled. Sean drew my hand up around his neck and then let go to haul me in close.

God, he felt amazing. Strong, powerful, and commanding. He was everything I needed and more, as I finally gave myself permission to really enjoy him.

Sliding my fingers through his hair, I angled my mouth for a deeper connection, and when a low growl left Sean's throat, my hips punched forward automatically.

"Shit." Sean tore his mouth free, his chest heaving against mine. He smoothed his hands down to my ass, and I knew exactly what he wanted.

I rocked forward, grinding my erection up against his. When his eyes slammed shut and his head fell back, I ran my hands up his chest and did it again.

"Fuck, that feels good."

It really did. Sean was hard all over, from his muscles to his cock, and as I continued to rub myself off on him, I was in real danger of never stopping. I slipped my hands underneath his shirt and began to inch it up. When I was just about halfway there, Sean's eyes reopened.

"You trying to get me naked, anchorman?"

I was curious what he would do if I said yes. There was no way in hell I'd ever get naked out here on the terrace. Too many lights from surrounding buildings, and too many windows for people to see from. But then again, he didn't have to get *naked* naked. Maybe just lose the shirt.

I licked my lower lip and looked down at the strip of skin I had revealed, and my cock began to throb a little harder.

"And if I said yes?"

Sean flashed a crooked smile then drew his shirt up over his head and tossed it down by his feet. I drank in all the naked skin he'd just revealed, and though I'd seen him a handful of times without his shirt on, this was the first time I could truly take pleasure in what I was seeing.

Wow, his body was so incredibly different from my own. Where I was tall and lean, and filled out my suits pretty nice, Sean had a rugged body, a rough-and-tumble, muscular body, with broad shoulders and built arms. He looked as though he could crash-tackle you to the ground after he'd chased you for miles. And suddenly all I could think about was how it would feel to be crash-tackled into bed.

I rubbed a hand over my aching shaft, but when Sean's hands went to the button of his cargo shorts, my brain quickly resurfaced.

"Uh, I don't think you should get naked out here. There's lots of—"

Sean laughed, and the sound was like stroking my very excited cock. "I'm not stripping."

"Oh, okay."

I wasn't sure if I was happy about that discovery or not. But when he flicked open the button of his shorts and said,

"I'm just getting more...comfortable," I took that as my cue to do the same.

"Come here." The order was given in that same authoritative tone Sean had used earlier, and then he reached for the hem of my shirt and drew me forward.

I flattened my hands against his chest. His skin was warm to the touch, and when he shivered, I lowered my head and drew my tongue across his right pec.

"Christ," he whispered, and when I scraped my teeth along the path I'd just licked, he trembled again.

Oh, I liked that. Somewhere, just beneath the surface, there was a vibrating tension that I couldn't wait for Sean to unleash. But until then, I'd happily tease it to the forefront.

I kissed my way up his neck, and then I reached down and rubbed the material covering his thick erection.

"*Ahh*, Xander."

I nipped at his earlobe. "Want me to stop?"

"Fuck no."

I chuckled and curled my fingers around him.

A strained sound left his lips as he punched his hips into my hand. I raised my head to look him in the eye, and his fiery stare sent flames licking along my skin.

That look was potent. It made me feel a little punch-drunk. "Tell me something you've noticed about me," I said. "Tell me something new."

Sean shakily exhaled as I gave him another slow stroke. Then he licked along his lower lip and traced his fingers along my jaw line.

"Your face. Jesus, Xander...it's, like, blinding. I never realized how fucking stunning you are."

My entire body leaned in to his, the desire radiating from him calling to me in the most primal of ways. "And now that you've noticed?"

Sean took my chin in hand and cocked his head to the side. "Now that I've noticed, you're all I see."

38

SEAN

WASN'T THAT THE damn truth?

Ever since my brain and body had locked on to Xander and really *seen* him, I'd found it impossible to see anything else. Not how it used to be, not how it might be—I was in the here and now, and the one thing I knew with absolute certainty was that the man currently massaging my cock was the sexiest person I'd ever seen in my life.

"I want you," I said, and it felt good to finally say it out loud. "I've had dreams where I've already *been* with you."

"What?" Xander's hand froze.

"Shocked?"

"Intrigued..."

I leaned down and said against his lips, "In my dream, though, your hand was *inside* my pants."

A wicked grin curved Xander's mouth as he let go and fingered my open shorts.

"Is that an invitation?"

I thrust my hips against him, making it clear that it was. Then I crushed my mouth down onto his, needing to taste him more than my next breath.

The instant our lips met, my body moved into action. I shoved off the rail and walked him back across the terrace, and as his back came up against the brick wall, Xander slipped his fingers behind the elastic of my boxers and finally curved his hand around my cock.

"Oh fuck yes," I said as I tore my mouth free.

"Of course you had to have a big cock." He smirked as he tightened his fist and drew it up my length, and the pleasure was so intense my toes curled and I squeezed my eyes shut. "Do you like it slow and hard, like this? Or quick pulls?"

I braced a hand on the bricks by his head, and once I was steady, I opened my eyes.

"Slow and hard?" Xander asked again. "Or fast and quick?"

I licked my lips, my dick pounding in his hand begging for some kind of release. "Any way you fucking want. Just don't stop."

Xander nipped at my lower lip then gave me a nice, solid tug and shoved his tongue deep inside my mouth. I groaned and jacked my hips forward, driving my shaft through his viselike grip. When he twisted his hand around the head of my cock, I grabbed his arm and slammed my body into his.

With every pump of my hips, Xander's hand moved faster and my breathing became more labored. I couldn't remember the last time I'd experienced pleasure this powerful. When he pulled his mouth free and kissed his way along my shoulder to the crook of my neck, I crowded in against him and began thrusting my hips as though I was deep inside him. A place I hadn't realized, until now, that I was dying to be.

"Xander..." I said, knowing I was really close to losing my shit. When he raised his head to respond, every single light in the near vicinity went out, and the world around us plunged into darkness.

"What the hell?"

"It's the heat..." Xander whispered across my lips, then he brushed his thumb over the swollen head of my cock, making my legs shake. "It's so hot that the grid short-circuited."

Oh fuck, if ever there'd been a more apt metaphor, I couldn't think of it.

I propelled my hips forward, grinding against the hand working me, and as my climax threatened, I burrowed my face into his neck. His scent—that same shampoo from the day before—flooded my senses, and as I kissed and sucked the warm skin, my hips picked up pace until I was fucking his hand.

I could hear his heavy breathing as he rubbed his hard cock on my thigh, and as the rush of pure ecstasy crashed down over us, everything in our bodies tensed.

"Xander—"

"*Sean...*"

My vision went blurry as blinding pleasure racked my

body, and as we came right there on Xander's *terrace*, I knew I'd never forget what it was called again.

As I drifted back down from such an incredible high, I raised my head to see how Xander was feeling. But it was difficult to make out his expression in the dark.

He didn't make me wait long, however. He pulled his hand free of my shorts and said, "Want to know what I've noticed about you most recently?"

"What's that?"

Xander ran a finger down the center of my chest, then he whispered against my lips, "Just how sexy you are when you come. Who knew, Detective *Dick*? Who knew?"

39

XANDER

THE FOLLOWING NIGHT as I stared at my reflection in the bathroom mirror, I brushed my fingers over the small purple bruise on my neck and thought back to the moment when Sean had given it to me. It'd been sometime before sunrise, the night had still been surrounding us where we lay on the couch in the great room, and I'd woken to his lips making their way up the side of my neck...

Damn. The memory was as delicious as the act itself. I smoothed my hand down over my chest to my heart and was more than aware it was now pounding a little harder.

I'd just spent the day making out with Sean. And as if he'd known I wouldn't be able to wrap my mind around that fact, he'd left proof of his presence in the most basic of ways.

I had no idea what was going on between us, and I'd stopped trying to guess. But somewhere during this nightmare of a situation, Sean had become my anchor. He'd become my port in the storm, and in some weird twist of fate, it appeared I had somehow become his.

My life was all upside down, and the only thing that made any kind of sense was the man I'd left out in my living room.

Knock, knock, knock.

"You okay in there?"

Okay, scratch that. The man who was now standing outside my bathroom door.

My lips curved, and all I could think was: when the hell did Sean become my reason to smile these days?

I pulled open the door to find Sean, barefoot and barechested, with a hand braced on the frame. Holy hell, with the way he filled out those sweats, it wasn't difficult to see why I'd given in and agreed to explore what we were feeling.

"Hello. Did you want something?" I asked.

"Maybe."

"Maybe, huh?" I trailed a hand down his ribs to the edge of his pants, and when he let go of the door to take hold of my wrist, I grinned. "Never took you for a liar."

Sean turned me so my back was up against the bathroom door and pinned my arm up against the wood. "I'm not lying. I *do* want something." He kissed his way up my jaw to my ear and whispered, "Your company. But that's not quite the way I was going to put it."

I turned my head, and our noses grazed. "Then how would you put it?"

"I missed you."

My stomach flipped, and when Sean's mouth found mine, I melted into his embrace. As I wound my arms around his neck, he deepened the kiss until a soft moan left me.

God, I couldn't seem to get enough of him.

"Are you sure we have to go tonight?" Sean said after he pulled his mouth free.

"Ah, okay. I understand now."

"You understand what?"

"That you came in here to try distract me with your body, so I'd forget about the awards tonight."

"I mean, I wish I'd thought of that," he said. "But there's only one reason I came in here, and that's because I woke up and you were gone."

I stared at his earnest expression then shook my head and sighed. "When did you learn to say all the right things?"

"I didn't."

"Trust me." I took his hands in mine. "You did."

Sean gave me a half-smile and took a step back to lean against the wall. "I'm still not getting out of this thing, am I?"

"I'm afraid not."

"Well, I suppose a date *is* kind of customary. I did let you get to second base, after all."

My mouth fell open. "*Let* me? I don't think so. And I already took you on a date. The steakhouse, remember?"

"Um, I paid, anchorman. So don't even try get off the hook."

Shit, he was right. He did pay for that meal, and it was hardly a date anyway. I'd still been trying to wrap my head around the fact that I was attracted to him, and had been self-conscious all night—then there was the hit-and-run.

It was hard to believe that had only been a few days ago when it felt like so much had changed. Well, when it came to Sean and me, that was.

"Okay, you're right. I guess I owe you a date, since I've all but stolen your virtue."

Sean trailed his eyes down my naked chest to my navy lounge pants. "Yeah, about that. You planning to actually let us *do* that at some point?"

Wide-eyed and slack-jawed, I stared at him for a moment, wondering if he meant that the way I was taking it. But judging from his heated look, I was starting to believe that Sean always dove in headfirst—hard and fast.

When I finally regained function of my brain, I said, "I think we should probably work up to it."

"The stealing of virtues? Or mine in particular?"

I bit down on the inside of my cheek to hold back my groan. Was he serious right now? "Would you stop saying it like that."

"Why? Do you not have any virtue left to steal?"

"Oh my God." I rubbed my face, and when Sean started to laugh, I glared at him, and he laughed even harder.

"I'm just fucking with you—or in this case, not yet."

Oh great, *now* he was coming up with the sex jokes.

"But you still owe me a date."

Deciding to ignore his "joke," I pushed right on. "Fair enough. How about I take you to an awards dinner?"

"Yeah, that'll do."

"Good. Now, I'm going to grab a quick shower."

"Is that an invitation?"

I shook my head. "Definitely not. You're going to go and have one in your room. I need to get ready, and that takes time."

"I'm sure it doesn't take *that* much time. You're pretty fucking perfect to begin with."

There he went again, saying all the right things. "Go."

Sean smirked as he backed out of the bathroom, his eyes trailing down to the erection I had no hope of controlling.

"You sure? I could help wash your...back."

My lips twitched, but I held on to my resolve and pointed to the door. "Get out."

Sean finally turned and strolled out of the en suite, and I found myself smiling again, all because of Sean Bailey.

I FINISHED KNOTTING my tie and took a final look at myself in the mirror, wondering how Sean was doing in the room next to mine. I hadn't heard a peep from him since he'd left me to shower, but as I did a final once-over and straightened the black bow tie, I had to admit I was eager to see how he had scrubbed up.

I picked up my phone and wallet, slipped them into my pockets, and made my way across the room, and when I opened the door, I stopped in my tracks.

Standing just outside his bedroom dressed in a perfectly fitted black tuxedo, Sean lounged casually against the door-frame with his legs crossed at the ankles, frowning at the cuff link he was trying to secure. His bow tie was hanging loose around his neck. When he heard me step out of the room and raised his head, my entire world came to a grinding halt.

Sean was absolutely breathtaking, handsome in the most classic of ways. As he pushed off the frame and straightened to his full height, I had to remind myself to breathe.

When I didn't immediately speak, he glanced down his body and then back to me.

"I look ridiculous, right?"

I licked my suddenly dry lips and took a step forward. "That's the last thing you look."

A smile slowly stretched his lips, and he went from handsome to devastating in a heartbeat.

"Do you need some help?" I gestured to the cuff links he held. He opened his palm, and I took them from him.

I slipped the first one through its holes and fastened it, and Sean stood there silent and steady. Once the second one was in place, I raised my eyes to his. His look made my heart long for things that neither of us were ready for.

Then he traced a thumb over my lips and said, "Blinding...I know I said it before but damn, Xander. You step into view and there's nothing but you."

40

SEAN

MY HAND SHOOK as I stared into Xander's beautiful eyes, and all I could think was: *I never want him to stop looking at me the way he is right now.*

"Thank you," he whispered as color bloomed on his cheeks, but it did nothing to detract from the elegant picture he made in a tuxedo that looked as though someone had sewn it onto him.

His bow tie was perfect, his suit jacket buttoned at the center, and his cuffs—unlike mine—were neat and fastened. He looked as at home in this outfit as he did in his shorts and shirt, and I'd never seen him look so stunning in all my life.

He touched the ends of the tie hanging around my neck and smiled.

"What?"

Like a kid caught with his hand in the cookie jar, Xander said, "Huh?"

"You were smiling. Why?"

Xander laughed softly and shook his head. "It's nothing."

"It's obviously something."

"Right. I was just thinking how instead of wanting to strangle you with this, I want to pull you to me and kiss the hell out of you instead."

"I wouldn't object."

"Hmm." His eyes fell to my lips. "I wouldn't either. But we need to leave if we're going to get there on time."

He began to tie the material, quickly and precisely, and once he was done, I buttoned my jacket over my holstered gun. "Ready?"

A frown appeared before Xander could shake it, and just as I was about to say something about it, he said, "Ready."

Deciding to let it go, I held out my hand and escorted him to the elevator.

I knew his response was to the weapon, but there was no way I was leaving without it. I'd gone over everything that Nichols had told me last night with Xander, and while I felt I was somehow failing him by having little to go on, the fact that I would be there tonight—along with backup—made me feel a little bit better.

We stepped out into the parking garage and headed for the SUV, and I noticed Xander tightening his hold on my hand.

"Hey," I said as I clicked the key fob and the lights blinked. "You're okay. I've got you."

Xander nodded but said nothing, and I couldn't blame

him. For a little while he'd been able to turn his brain off and forget about always having to watch his back. But now that he was out in the open again, I knew that—just like me—he was wondering who *else* was watching it.

I pulled open the door and waited until he was buckled in before shutting it. Then I booked it around the front and climbed in beside him. I looked over to see him wiping his hands nervously on his thighs, and I hated that I couldn't ease that worry, take away that fear. The one thing I could do, however, was make sure he stayed safe.

I reached over and placed my hand on top of his, and when Xander turned my way, I smiled and thought that maybe if I got him talking it would get his mind off other, scarier things.

"So, you never told me what awards you're up for tonight, Mr. Big Shot Anchorman. Just that there's—how many? Five?"

"Try three."

"My mistake. I just thought with you being so famous and all..."

Xander laughed as I pulled out onto the main road and headed toward the Fairmont Hotel, where the awards dinner was being held in the Millennium Park Conference Center.

"Mhmm, *so* famous. But to answer your question, the news team is up for an innovative storytelling award, and I'm up for the two solo ones. One for excellence in broadcast journalism, and the other is distinguished reporting."

"Ahh." I winked at him. "Very fancy."

"Fits my upper-class ways, don't you think?"

I let my eyes wander down over him and nodded. "It does. You're a shoo-in for sure. Definitely looking *very* distinguished tonight."

Xander smiled. "Thank you for letting me go tonight."

"Of course. It's important to you."

"It is. You know, I've never taken anyone to these awards with me before. But I'm glad it's you I get to share this with."

My heart nearly tripped over itself, and before I knew I was going to ask, I said, "And which *me* are you sharing it with? Bodyguard? Fake boyfriend? Or..."

Xander squeezed my hand. "I don't think it really matters anymore. Bodyguard, fake boyfriend, or whatever else you might be to me. It's *you* that I'm here sharing it with, and I've never seen you look more handsome than you do tonight."

He was right. What was in a few details when the most important ones were clear? It was him and me tonight, whatever version we wanted to be, and right now, that was good enough for me.

41

XANDER

"XANDER! XANDER! OVER here!"

I looked through the sea of cocktail dresses and tuxedos and saw Ryan madly waving from a table toward the front.

We'd arrived with about five minutes to spare, and with the room close to capacity, it was going to be a long journey from one end of the decked-out space to the other. With a stage upfront and purple drapes lining the walls on all sides, the soft glow of the lights, and gold table and chair settings, gave an elegant feel to the place.

I took in a deep breath and tried to calm my nerves. They'd almost gotten the better of me back at my place when I saw Sean's gun. But the drive over here had given me time to compose myself, and to remember that I wasn't in this alone.

Something I was made very aware of when Sean said by my ear, "That our table over there?"

I nodded, but the grimace on my face must have relayed how excited I was about the prospect of getting to it.

"Stop worrying," Sean said. "I told you, I've got you tonight."

When his fingers tightened around mine, I felt an immediate sense of calm wash over me.

"Okay, anchorman, let's go." Sean interlaced his fingers through mine and then headed off, and as the small gatherings at each table shifted to let us by, I knew that whatever look he had on his face was enough to keep anyone who was slightly curious about him from approaching.

That worked for me. There was nothing I hated more than gossip, and with everything else going on tonight, the last thing I wanted to do was explain or lie about Sean.

We were almost home free—about two tables from where Ryan and Cynthia were grinning at me like a pair of fools—when Benton Hale moved directly into Sean's path.

Stupid, stupid *man*. That wasn't an entirely accurate statement. Benton Hale was very smart. But anyone who stepped in front of Sean when he was on a mission made me wonder how well his or her brain could possibly be functioning.

"Xander, I was hoping to see you here tonight." Benton had to practically crane his head around Sean's shoulder to greet me. "I see you brought a date."

Sean looked in my direction, and the expression on his face screamed one thing: *Who the fuck is this?*

I gave a quick wave to Benton, loathing the idea of doing

the introduction spiel, but then the lights flashed, indicating it was time to be seated.

Oh, thank you, God.

"Sorry we can't stay and chat, Benton," I said, and then looked to Sean. "We need to go and find our seats."

Seeming to get my not-so-subtle hint, Sean turned to Benton and said, "You mind moving?"

The look on Benton's face was comical, to say the least. It was clear that Sean had no idea who Benton was, and I knew that lack of recognition was killing him.

Clearly not willing to make a scene, Benton stepped aside, and Sean plowed ahead, tugging me behind him.

When we finally reached our destination, Ryan and Cynthia, both of whom had flown solo tonight, greeted us with a smile. Jim and his wife Kelly said their hellos from the opposite side of the table.

Marcus was standing off to the side deep in conversation with Luis Kozlowski, the president of ABC's news division, and when the lights flashed for a second time, Sean let go of my hand and pulled out the seat in front of me.

Look at him, playing up the gentleman card.

"Thank you," I said as I took my seat and he slid into the one beside me.

"For rescuing you from Benton Hale? You're fucking welcome. I know about all I need to when it comes to him. He's on your list."

Oh, that's right.

"What a stuck-up name. *Benton.*"

"That's *not* what I was thanking you for," I said, shaking my head. "I was thanking you for navigating that mess and pulling my chair out for me."

Sean winked. "Hey, what can I say? Apparently the tux brings out the gentleman in me."

"Except around Benton."

"Can you please stop saying his fucking name?"

I smirked and looked to the stage, where I could see the host off to the side reading through his cue cards. Waiters bustled around the tables offering glasses of red or white wine to guests, and when Marcus finally took his seat, he looked at the two of us and gave a curt nod.

"Evening, Alexander."

"Evening," I said, and wondered why he hadn't bothered greeting Sean. Then I remembered that no one here was aware that they knew each other. Jesus, I was so bad at this fake undercover stuff. The only reason I was doing a decent job of the boyfriend part was because tonight it actually felt like Sean was my—

Okay, it was probably best not to go there right now with everything else going on. *One thing at a time, Xander. Get through the awards. Get home safely. And then maybe think about the fact that you wouldn't mind if Sean never stopped holding your hand.*

"Marcus, this is Sean. My date," I finally said. Sean stood to hold his hand out, and Marcus shook it.

"It's nice to meet you, Sean. This is the first time Alexander's ever brought someone to this ceremony. You must be someone he wants to impress."

Everyone at the table laughed. Sean took a seat and aimed a grin my way. "There's no need for that. I'm already impressed."

Out of the corner of my eye, I saw Ryan place a hand to his chest and fake-swoon beside Cynthia. If I were close enough to kick him, I would've.

"So," Cynthia said, leaning across the table and snagging Sean's attention. "How long have the two of you known each other?"

As Sean went about answering that doozy of a question, a waiter stepped between the two of us and held up the bottles of wine.

"Red or white, sir?"

I decided on the Merlot, and when he smiled and began to fill my glass, I couldn't help but think I'd seen him somewhere before.

"Isn't that right, Xander?"

At the sound of Jim's voice, I tuned back into the conversation going on around me.

"He's already won the *distinguished* reporter award. So the real golden goose here tonight is the Frederick L. Hutcheon Editor Award. We've all placed bets. I have great faith in you."

I nodded along, still slightly distracted, and when the waiter moved on to the next table, Sean squeezed my thigh.

"Everything okay?" he asked, dark eyes searching my face.

I quickly shoved aside my wayward thoughts, determined to enjoy myself. "Everything's fine." I reached for my glass and took a sip of the smooth red. "I'm just trying to work out how to break it to him that I'm not up for the Frederick L. Hutcheon Editor Award this year. He's going to be a little bit poorer come the morning."

42
===

SEAN

WHY DID AWARD ceremonies always have to be so long and tedious? I'd never been one to watch them on TV, and as I sat there—twenty minutes in—I was starting to remember why.

The first problem was that they always followed the same template. A host who told the bad jokes, the audience who felt they had to laugh, and the thank-you speeches that were always rushed to fit into the allotted network segment.

Unless, of course, the award ceremony wasn't broad-casted—then you just had to sit through the loooong speeches.

It wouldn't be so bad if I could partake in the free drinks. But there was no way in hell I was touching a drop tonight, not when my focus was one hundred percent on the man to my left.

When we'd arrived, I'd spotted Nichols making nice at a table in the rear, which worked out well, since I was now at the front. The guy didn't clean up too bad, all in all, but it didn't escape my notice that he'd opted for a plain suit as opposed to the penguin getup.

I had a feeling I'd be getting shit for years when he reported back to the guys just how spruced up I was. But I didn't really care. I'd wear a fucking tutu if that was what it took to keep Xander safe.

So far, things appeared to be going along fairly smoothly. Jim had apparently decided I passed whatever little test he'd given me the other day, and Marcus either had his phone to his ear or a droll look on his face that made me think I should send my untouched wine *his* way.

The person I was most interested in, however, had my hand in his, a small smile on his lips as he listened to the latest winner as though he knew every single one of the bazillion people she was up there thanking.

But that was just like Xander. He was always so personable, and had a smile or story to help brighten a person's day. It was no surprise he was one of the most watched TV news anchors in the country. He was charming, affable, and really fucking easy on the eyes.

So much so that I leaned in and said, "I can't wait to get home with you tonight."

Xander whipped his head in my direction. When I waggled my eyebrows, he glanced around the table to make sure no one was listening.

He was in luck: they were riveted by the host who had just stepped back onto the stage.

"Have you been drinking?"

I smirked, because Xander knew I wouldn't touch a thing while I was on watch.

"Nope. I've been sitting here thinking about the way your voice gets all breathy when you're turned on." I inched my hand up his thigh, and Xander licked at his lower lip. "I wonder how it would sound right now."

He pressed his hand down over the top of mine, slowly drew it up higher, then sat back in his chair and faced the stage. "If I'm lucky, you're about to find out."

My eyes returned to the host as he took his spot behind the podium.

"The nominees for the Excellence in Broadcast Journalism Award this year are: John Hamby from CBS, Pete Collier from FOX News, Sharon Elmhurst from PBS, and Alexander Thorne from ENN."

As everyone at the table clapped and gave Xander the thumbs-up, the hair on the back of my neck stood tall and I scanned the room, looking for Nichols, who I spotted in his seat watching the crowd.

Good, that was good. As my eyes came back to the table, I saw Xander looking at me and forced a smile.

"Good luck," I said, not wanting to worry him, but this was the moment I'd been dreading all night. The chance that he might win, and that I'd have to let him move further than touching distance away from me.

Xander flashed that famous smile, then looked to the stage as the host announced, "The winner is Alexander Thorne with ENN."

Our table erupted with applause, and everyone jumped to their feet in celebration.

Xander got to his feet. I hugged him in close and whispered, "Congratulations, anchorman. Go get your fancy award. I've got you."

I ordered myself to let him go, gave him a quick nod, then stepped aside. My eyes darted from person to person as he drew closer to the stage, then a flash of movement caught my eye. One of the waiters rushed him from the side of the stage and tackled Xander to the ground, where he hit the stairs hard—and chaos erupted.

I charged toward the front of the room, shoving people out of my path. When I reached the motherfucker who'd knocked Xander out cold, I saw the flash of a knife.

I grabbed the fucker by his hair and shoulder and hauled him off Xander with so much force that the two of us stumbled back into each other. He quickly got his footing and spun around, swiping the knife through the air with savage intensity.

I managed to sidestep each reckless swipe as he snarled, "He's mine!" and the second I saw his face, I placed him: the guy who had been cleaning the doors to Xander's building.

He lunged forward again, thrusting the blade with killer intent. I grabbed his wrist in an attempt to disarm him, and we grappled for dominance.

People screamed and ran from the room, some calling for help while others seemed to freak the fuck out. I rammed the guy backward into the table behind him.

There was no way to get to my gun, so I twisted his arm

with the knife at an ugly angle and landed a blow to his side. He howled in pain but then seemed to get another surge of adrenaline. He struggled to get free, and his sweaty wrist slipped from my grip. Then he launched himself forward and plunged the knife deep into my side.

Searing pain tore through me as he pulled it free, and I stumbled back into the table behind me, my vision blurring. The screams were much fainter now as the ballroom emptied, but I could hear Nichols shouting, "Get the fuck out of the way!" as I clutched at my side and blinked, trying to see Xander.

Braced against the table, I shoved my jacket aside to reach for my gun, and as I finally zeroed in on Xander, I saw him getting to his feet. As he turned around and spotted me, his face paled, and that was when I saw his attacker make his move—a second later, I fired off the kill shot.

43

XANDER

THE SOUND OF a gunshot echoing around the ballroom made my entire body freeze, as my attacker stiffened and fell lifeless to the ground.

Oh my God. Oh my fucking God. Blood oozed out of the hole in the back of the man's shirt, and it took a second to compute that he was dead. As in, really, *really* dead. But then I heard the loud crash of a table and all that was on it hitting the floor, and I jerked my head up to see Sean keeling over.

"Sean!" I shouted, and ran to his side. When I reached him and saw a stain spreading across his shirt, I dropped to my knees and applied pressure to the wound.

"Xander..."

"Help!" I called out at the top of my lungs as I looked around the room. People had begun trickling back inside now, but the fear on their faces seemed to hold their feet hostage.

"Someone call 911!" A man nodded at me and turned on his heel, and I watched him book it out of the room.

Sean reached down to where my hands were now covered in his blood, and I shook my head.

"Don't touch, just keep talking," I said, having no idea what to say.

"Is he dead?"

Of course that was the first thing Sean wanted to know.

"I didn't stop to check a pulse, but...yes, I'm pretty sure he's dead."

"Good. Now you'll be safe." Sean coughed, and as more blood spilled from under my hand, I kept my eyes on his.

"I'm always safe with you."

"Yeah, but in case I don't—"

"No," I interrupted, my eyes beginning to blur. "We're not doing that."

Sean gave a pained half-smile. "We're not?"

"No. We're not." I reached for his hand and squeezed his fingers, trying to give him an ounce of the reassurance his touch always gave me.

"Xander?"

"Yes?"

His breathing hitched and faltered, and when a fit of coughs erupted from his chest, his fingers tightened around mine with crushing force.

"Tell Bailey and Kieran that I'm sorry I wasn't better, okay?"

Tears fell down my cheeks as I desperately looked around, hoping by some miracle that the ambulance was here. But when all I saw were the desolate faces of my friends and colleagues, I turned back to Sean and again shook my head, my denial strong as I looked down into his fading eyes.

"I won't do that. You're going to be fine. Okay?"

Sean pulled his hand free and reached up to gently run his fingers across my wet cheek. I had to bite into my lip to keep from totally losing it.

"Blinding," he whispered, as his hand fell back to his side. "You stepped into view, and now there's nothing but you. Blinding..."

No, no, no, my mind screamed as his eyes fell shut, and I reached for his hand again. When I got no response, I crowded down over him and kissed his pale lips, then I began to shake from the sorrow overtaking me. This couldn't be happening. It couldn't be.

When the paramedics finally rushed in and pried our hands apart, I felt as though they were ripping my heart clear out of my chest.

How was I ever going to get through another day without feeling his hand in mine? The answer was as simple as it was devastating—I wasn't sure I could.

THANK YOU

Thank you for reading INSIDE AFFAIR. I hope you enjoyed watching the sparks fly between these two unlikely characters!

Make sure to join me for the next book in Xander and Sean's journey, BREAKING NEWS, as they discover the new affection they share now runs much deeper than either of them suspected.

You can pre-order BREAKING NEWS here!

Release Date: July 27th, 2020

**Love INSIDE AFFAIR? Leave a review!
Reviews are vital to authors, and all reviews, even just a couple of quick sentences, can help a reader decide whether to pick up our books.

*If you enjoyed this book, please consider leaving a review on the site you purchased from.***

ABOUT THE AUTHOR

If you'd like to get to know Ella better, you can find her getting up to all kinds of shenanigans at:

The Naughty Umbrella

And if you would like to talk with other readers who love Ella's character's from her Chicagoverse, you can find them **HERE** at
Ella Frank's Temptation Series Facebook Group.

Ella Frank is the *USA Today* Bestselling author of the Temptation series, including Try, Take, and Trust and is the co-author of the fan-favorite contemporary romance, Sex Addict. Her Exquisite series has been praised as "scorching hot!" and "enticingly sexy!"

Some of her favorite authors include Tiffany Reisz, Kresley Cole, Riley Hart, J.R. Ward, Erika Wilde, Gena Showalter, and Carly Philips.

Want to stay up to date with all things Ella?
You can sign up here to join her newsletter

Printed in Great Britain
by Amazon

82814779R00164